To Margi

The Weight of Innocence

The Weight of Innocence

J. A. De Yoe

Library of Congress Control Number:		2012909562
ISBN:	Hardcover	978-1-4771-1910-5
	Softcover	978-1-4771-1909-9
	Ebook	978-1-4771-1911-2

This book was printed in the United States of America.

To order additional copies of this book, contact:
Xlibris Corporation
1-888-795-4274
www.Xlibris.com
Orders@Xlibris.com
111535

1

The warm air worked as a poultice, pulling the winter frost from the hibernating earth. Fog shrouded everything as we sliced our passage through this thick curtain. Its density turned our voices into ghostly whispers.

My two younger brothers, Paul and Peter, and I leaned our small frames, headfirst, into the heavy smokelike air. We clutched our books firmly to our chests in a futile attempt to keep out the dampness. As if by osmosis, the dampness penetrated, ignoring clothes and skin, making bones and teeth rattle.

We sensed our way across the arena parking lot, only sure of our location when we were close to the building that served as a venue for most of the public gatherings in our little community.

"Look," said Paul. "The door is open."

There was a warm glow filling the doorway, ending at the sill, the light not strong enough to pierce the fog outside. A promise of warmth and our own curiosity pulled us in. There was an eerie muffled hush that echoed, and having nowhere to go, the silence bounced back to the source.

As we moved into the building, the air thinned, and the thick absolute quiet faded to the hollow silence of a near-empty building. We were alone in the building, and we moved in hesitantly, away from the doorway, away from the soul-numbing cold.

The concession stand was shuttered and locked. Peering through the glass in the doors to the rink area, we saw only darkness, and we were too cold to be tempted to try the ice. We investigated the ladies' washroom to explore the mysteries held within. Except for the lack of urinals and the addition of a vending machine with products we had all seen under the bathroom sink at home, it seemed that there was little to offer in the form of entertainment. We wandered back into the hallway, and as we were about to leave, Peter, my nine-year-old brother, pointed to the stairs.

"What's up there?" he asked.

"Let's see," I suggested, not waiting for an answer but heading up the stairs.

At the top of the stairs, an unlocked door greeted us, and we accepted the invitation to enter. The large assembly hall was lined with stackable chairs and long tables. At one end of the room, sitting on a table was a clear plastic box filled with bingo balls. The box had a switch and a plug, and when turned on, air pumped into the box, making the balls jump, forcing a single ball into a compartment at the top of the box. This niche was open at one side of the box, enabling the ball's removal. We took the top off of the box and discovered that the balls would fly unrestrainedly about the room when turned on.

When it was clear that no one was going to come and throw us out, we pelted the balls at each other, rolled around on the floor, laughing—school forgotten.

I left my brothers and went to explore the rest of the room. I discovered several cases of Coke. We drank thirstily until we were totally sated and bloated with gas; then I shook up what was left in my bottle and sprayed Peter. Of course, he retaliated. Paul, never one to be left out, got in on the action. It was two against one. I armed myself with a new bottle, and the war was on. The three of us were covered in the sticky, syrupy mess, and we slid on the Coke-drenched floor and watched the brown liquid drip from the ceiling and down the walls.

At eleven, nine, and seven, doing something forbidden usually called for adult interference before terminating the activity. However, we grew tired of all the foreign pleasures that the arena could offer and headed home with some regret, knowing that freedom like this would not present itself again soon. We took a case of Coke with us as a memento and were able to enter our house unnoticed. We hid our cache in the closet of our room.

2

Mama was an astute businesswoman. She overcame hurdles that would have stopped most women and didn't let life's little roadblocks get in her way. She was a survivor through necessity, having been dealt seven children and a husband who had deserted her when the youngest was only a few months old.

For five years after my father made his exodus, she struggled alone financially doing factory work and waiting on tables in a diner in Welford. A turning point for her was the day the cook at the diner got sick and didn't show up for work. That day, her boss, Mr. Peters, said that he would wait on the customers and Mama would have to take over in the kitchen. Having so many kids had well qualified her to cook up fast and easy meals. The regular customers raved about her cooking, and Mr. Peters asked her to take on the job permanently. Mama said that she would have to think about it since the job offered the same pay as waiting on tables, but she would lose her tips.

When she arrived home and told us of the offer, it was clear that she would rather cook than work in the factory or wait on tables, but her income would decrease, and she wasn't earning enough to make ends meet as it was. She always seemed to be one step behind in payments.

"Robbing Peter to pay Paul," she would say with a smile, looking at my two brothers.

Her eyes lit up when she told us of the compliments she had received, and she talked of the things that she would like to add to the menu.

Jacquelyn, my oldest sister, told her that she should take the job, and we all agreed that Mama's life seemed to consist of only work and sleep.

As a child, you are often asked what you want to be when you grow up. It seemed that Mama did not want to be what she was, and we must have realized, even then, that if Mama was a cook, she would be allowed to be what she wanted to be.

My sisters helped with a lot of the housework, and my older brothers had part-time jobs that helped buy some of their clothes and extras like skates and baseball gloves. This aid did not eliminate any of Mama's costs, and she had to work just as much since, when they were old enough to have jobs, the cost of their sports and clothes seemed to grow to meet their wages. Jacquelyn strengthened her argument, saying that she would be finished school in just a few months, and she already had a job lined up, eliminating the expense of one dependent, and that she was going to get married the following autumn.

Rachel, the second eldest, piped in, saying that she would take on more babysitting and be able to purchase her own clothes. My brothers Henri and Alexi encouraged her to talk to Mr. Peters. We realized that our life would be happier if Mama was content in what she was doing.

She was not convinced that we could get by on any less income than we already had, and she had pretty much made up her mind to turn down the offer when the phone rang.

Jacquelyn ran to answer as she always did, thinking that her beau was on the other end. A moment later, she returned to the kitchen and said, "Mama, it's Mr. Peters. Tell him you'll take the job."

Mama went to the phone in the front hall, and we all followed to hear what she would say.

"Hello," she said as she lifted the receiver.

There was a pause while she listened, and then she said, "I am really tempted, Mr. Peters, because I really enjoyed cooking. But to be honest with you, I can't afford to give up my factory wage, which is twenty-five cents more an hour, and I lose the tips I get from waiting on tables when I am in the kitchen."

She listened again for a minute and smiled at us. Her eyes lit up, and she spoke into the phone again. "In that case, I will have to give my notice of one week, but I can work on the weekend and start officially on Wednesday next week."

She hung up the phone, and we all started asking questions at once. "What happened? Are you going to work for him? Can you quit the factory?"

"He said that he would give me five cents an hour more than the factory and that all the tips will be shared!" She seemed so utterly surprised and pleased that we all cheered.

Mama took to cooking like a retriever to water. She came home with ideas for menu items and talked of things she had changed in the kitchen to make working in it easier. She complained about the mess and dirt left behind by the former cook. Mr. Peters was happy, and his clientele was growing. Her portion of the tips grew with the business, and she was able to buy herself some new clothes. She even went to a hairdresser and had her hair cut properly.

A new vitality that we had never before witnessed emerged in her. She had Sundays off, and even when she worked a long day, she did not seem tired. It was as if life had become a pleasure instead of a drudge.

Mama even had a gentleman call. She met him in the diner. He worked up north in a logging camp, and he came down once every three weeks for five days. I had mixed feelings about him, since he really didn't try to make friends with me, or my siblings for that matter. He did put on a show in front of Mama, of making a fuss over Paul, the baby. He was not unkind to us—merely uninterested.

He met her at her work and raved about her cooking. Maurice was his name. He was only a little taller than Mama—around five feet four inches, bald as a worm, and stocky. He was also very strong. One time, Mr. Peters stopped at the house for a drink, and he fell as he went down the front steps. Maurice scooped him off the ground and carried him back into the house and sat him on the couch. It turned out that Mr. Peters had only turned his ankle, but Maurice's breathing didn't even speed up. I guess his muscles were a result of his line of work.

I might have been a little jealous of Maurice and very leery of any man who might hurt my mother. I remember hearing her cry many nights after my father had first gone. For Mama, life had turned around from a dismal existence to happy contentment, even though she still worked very hard.

About a year after she had been cooking, Mr. Peters told Mama that the city was going to demolish the building that housed the diner. Within six months, the diner would close, and he had no intention of finding another location. He said that his customers would not follow to another area, and there was nothing within the area that he could afford. He was getting up in years anyway and felt he could afford to retire.

Mama was devastated, and we didn't know what to do to help her. Jacquelyn had gotten married the previous year, and she was the only one who seemed to be able to talk to Mama on an equal level. The rest of us felt helpless as we watched her distress.

Maurice phoned Mama once a week when he was out of town. Shortly after this blow, I overheard Mama talking to him about her pending unemployment. They talked a long time that night, so I was surprised when I answered the phone the next night, and it was Maurice again. I listened at the kitchen door to hear what was being said, but Mama was doing more listening than talking, and her responses gave me no clue to what was being said. When she finished using the phone, she went and sat in the dark living room.

About a week later, when we were all sitting around the table in the kitchen, dunking some of her famous hermit cookies in milk, she told us of the plan Maurice had proposed.

"In six months, I will be out of work. Maurice has talked to his boss in the logging camp, and it turns out that they need a cook for the loggers." She talked fast so that we could not interrupt her until she had finished her spiel. "His boss is willing to give me a job for a lot more money than I am making now, and we can rent a house there cheaply. He says there is a two-story house, larger than this one, for rent. I have thought about it, and I want to go and look at it. If it is as good as it sounds, I think that we should move."

"We can't! I have to graduate here! I only have four months left of school!" Rachel wailed. "What about Tommy?" Tommy was her latest in a long parade of beaus.

Henry and Alexi looked at each other, and Henry said, "What about our jobs? What about school?' He was serious about school and had no intention of becoming a laborer.

"Of course," Mama said, seemingly relieved to have a question for which she had a positive answer. "They have schools up there just like they do here. You don't think I would let you go without finishing your schooling after what we have had to live through because of my lack of education, do you?"

She looked at all of us and said, "There is a school for grades one to five, another school for grades six to nine. Alexi will go there for a year. A third school, that Henri will be bussed to, is a high school eight miles away.

It goes to grade thirteen. Maybe you and Alexi can get part-time jobs in the camp, but the difference in my pay will cover the cost of your extras, and maybe I can even give you an allowance." She didn't seem as positive about this though.

She looked tired and stubborn. You didn't argue with her in this mood because you wouldn't win, and so far, she had done what she thought would be best for her family. We had to assume that she would continue to do so. Rachel was the only one with any real objections.

I thought it might be fun to live somewhere else; my only fear was alleviated when I asked, "Will we be living with Maurice?"

"No," my mother said quickly, "at least not now. What future he and I might have, I don't know. This isn't about Maurice and me. It is about how we are going to survive and how I am going to support us."

She didn't say the word "marriage," and I hoped it wouldn't happen.

"You will have to let me decide after I've seen the place. I am going up there next weekend on the train to Timmins, and Maurice will pick me up there and drive me to the camp in Auburn. I will ask for Saturday off, leave Friday night, and return Sunday. Maurice will pay for my ticket, and I will meet his boss. Rachel, you will babysit. There is no sense in asking me any more questions until I know the answers."

Her decision was made, and there was no more discussion. She left us and went up to her bedroom.

Rachel headed straight to the phone and called Jacquelyn and started crying to her about not wanting to move. It seemed that Jacquelyn already knew all about it, and she told Rachel that she had talked to Mama about Rachel finishing her school in Welford and staying with Jacquelyn and her new husband.

Rachel's whole attitude changed, and now she seemed to think we should move, probably anticipating more freedom from rules and more time with Tommy or his successor.

3

Mama returned from her weekend expedition ecstatic and happy. Her excitement was infectious, and we all agreed with enthusiasm that we should move. I looked forward to the new adventure and exploring unknown places. "Up north" sounded to me like another country. My younger brothers were responding to everyone else's anticipation, and my older brothers, although more subdued, didn't mind. Henri was fourteen, and Alexi was thirteen.

Rachel and Mama had a little tearful scene when Mama gave her the choice of staying with Jacquelyn or coming with us. Rachel, of course, chose to stay, and although I knew she was looking forward to having more freedom, she was a little frightened at having Mama so far away.

After all the good-byes and tears a month later, we packed our belongings and crowded into Maurice's car and the moving truck. Maurice drove the rented truck, and Mama drove his car. We left early in the morning and arrived after three the next morning. We were all asleep when we stopped in front of a big white clapboard house. The ground was covered in snow, but the walk and the driveway had been cleared. We woke up long enough to take some small possessions and have our beds made up. It was cold outside, but the house was warm that March night. Maurice had lit the furnace and shoveled snow before coming down to get us.

The aroma of freshly brewed coffee greeted us when we woke in the morning. Since Mama didn't drink coffee, I assumed that Maurice was still here. I couldn't imagine her having guests, since she didn't know anyone except Maurice. We came down the stairs and found that the furniture had been positioned, there were no boxes to be seen, and there were even curtains hanging on the windows. Mama and Maurice had worked all night unloading and unpacking.

There, in the center of the huge yellow kitchen, stood a massive oval pine table. It was not new, and the wood was scarred in many spots with water rings from glasses. White spots in the wood indicated that something too hot had been placed on it. Two leaves were in place, and around the sides of the table were ornate carvings. The legs had heavy claws at the bottom that reminded me of lion's paws. It was beautiful! It was surrounded by eight high-backed chairs. The carved pattern was repeated on the back of each chair.

"Where did we get the table?" asked Alexi.

"It was left with the house. Maybe the people who were here were moving somewhere smaller and didn't have space for it. The landlord said we could have it." As she said this, Mama ran her hand over the surface. "It may not look like much now, but when I sand down the top and put some varnish on it, I think it will be beautiful." Fatigue didn't disguise the fact that she was happy.

We all agreed that it was far nicer than the Formica table we had before.

"This will be a brand new start for us, and I think that we will have good luck here." She turned and smiled at Maurice while she was speaking, and it seemed that something secret passed between them as they looked at each other. I got a funny feeling in my stomach that I couldn't identify. I quickly squashed it, not wanting anything to spoil the excitement of our new home and new life.

Mama started to make some oatmeal, and we explored our new environment. The kitchen was at the back of the house. It was almost as wide as the house, except for a small bathroom on the south side. From the driveway, you could come into the mudroom that had been added on the original structure. The driveway was on the north side of the house.

The door to the basement was on this side of the kitchen. This stairway was placed below the stairs going up to the second floor. Ruffled yellow and white curtains were tied back at the sides of the window in front of the kitchen sinks. On the other side of the window was a veranda whose roof was high enough not to block the view of a wonderful treed backyard.

There was no shortage of cupboards and counters in the kitchen. Peeking into the cupboards, I found that our kitchen things had already found a home. The brand new fridge standing against the south wall had been a gift from Mr. Peters. On the wall away from the window was a swinging door that led to the dining room. A shiny brass plate protected the paint from dirty hand prints. Next to that was a black cast iron wood stove already employed, burning the cardboard boxes that had transported our possession.

We roamed around, and went back through the door from the kitchen into the long front hallway. As you faced the front door, the stairs were on your left. An archway opened to your right into the combination living and dining room. This room was about twenty eight-feet long and eighteen-feet wide. A large bay window looked out onto the front yard and snow-covered bushes grew directly beneath the window. Along the south side, a stone fireplace reached the ceiling and on either side was a long narrow window.

At the dining room end, a built-in window bench sat in front of a bowed window, and on the back wall, the swinging door went back to the kitchen. We didn't have enough furniture to fill the room. Our old kitchen table seemed out of place in the dining room, but the windows were beautiful with the new floral drapes that I had seen Mama making before we moved. Her old, hand-me-down sewing machine stood by the swinging door, in readiness to serve at a moment's notice. Mama was not only the world's greatest cook, she could sew almost anything and was forever mending our jeans and shirts, getting every breath of life out of them that she could.

We raced upstairs to a six-foot square landing. The largest bedroom was in front, facing east, taking up the width of the house except the space taken up by the stairwell. Paul, Peter, and I were assigned this room. There were still unpacked boxes of clothes in our room, but our beds and dressers were neatly arranged. I slept on the top bunk above Paul, and Peter had the second bunk bed to himself. He liked the bottom. I must have been very tired when we arrived because I hadn't heard them putting the furniture in our room. They must have however, since only the beds were there when I went to sleep. The two windows in our room had green roll up blinds. They must have been left behind by the previous tenants.

The bathroom was black and white. The walls had a fresh coat of white enamel paint. Black and white covered the floor and looked like a checkerboard. Funny-looking faucets were installed in the large, claw-footed bathtub. The taps were small, and the spout was very tiny. Attached to the spout was a white hose with a nozzle that looked like a shower head. The sink sat on a pedestal.

The morning light was starting to filter through the frosted window on the south side of the house. We found a strange box next to the toilet. When we lifted the lid, we saw only darkness; it was bottomless! Paul was too big to fit, so we didn't find out until after our explorations that this was a laundry chute that dropped down to the basement.

The other two bedrooms were across the back of the house, one larger than the other. Mama's room was the smallest, and Henri and Alexi had the medium-sized bedroom. Mama's closet had a secret door hidden in the back wall. Through that door, we found that there were stairs going up to the attic. Ascending these, we entered a square room that reached the outside walls of the house. Wide wooden planks covered the floor, and the ceiling sloped down like a pyramid under the roof. A gable at the front of the attic housed a window that had twelve square panes of glass. Through that window, we looked over our new neighborhood. We looked down on the houses and could see a school and a large building that turned out to be the arena. Our house seemed to be the largest and tallest one in sight. At the time, that seemed to be a very important fact to me.

Trees stood bare and slanted streaks of sunlight were starting to make their way into the front yard. A tidy, white picket fence surrounded the garden, and a massive maple stood in the center of the lawn. Agreeing that the attic would make a wonderful hideout, we ran downstairs and excitedly told Mama that we loved our new home, asked her about the box in the bathroom, and told her that we wanted to make the attic into a hideout.

She was pleased that we had approved of her choice and said that she would think about the hideout, since it would involve disruption of her room and closet every time we wanted to use it. She explained that her room was the only space she had to be alone.

"We'll trade you rooms, Mama," said Henri, who had been very quiet until now. Alexi nodded in agreement.

"My room isn't as big as your room, you know," said Mama as she thought about it.

"We can stack our beds. They are bunk beds after all, and we don't have to have them separate Maybe, we could even move our beds up to the attic." Alexi said, getting excited as he thought about it.

"Well, I don't think that that would be a very good idea in the winter time," laughed Maurice. "There isn't any heat up there."

I resented his intrusion. He had nothing to do with this. I didn't say anything, but I stuck my tongue out at him when he was looking the other way.

Breakfast was ready, and Mama was dishing out the porridge with a contented, though tired smile on her face. "I'll change rooms with you," she said, "But Maurice is right, you can't sleep in the attic in the winter. Maybe you could use it in the summer, as long as I don't hear a lot of noise over my head when I'm trying to sleep."

After breakfast, we went down to the basement, which didn't have much of interest other than pipes, wires, plumbing for laundry and an oil furnace.

Mama had sent a letter ahead, saying that we would be attending the three different schools, so when we arrived at the right schools on Monday, we were expected. Each of us was in a different grade, but Peter was in the same classroom as Paul, and the three of us attended the same school.

Most of the students were French Canadians. Since we were raised in Southern Ontario, we spoke both French and English. My mother was French, and we spoke that mostly at home, but English couldn't help but creep in at times since that is what we were exposed to at school and outside of our home. Our classes were taught mostly in French, except English of course.

None of us had any trouble fitting in. Being the "new kids" had many advantages. You could drop any of your history that you chose—something that you couldn't do if you stayed in the same place from the time you were born. If you were a crybaby in kindergarten, people thought you were still a baby when you were in grade five. Peter had always taken a lot of taunting and now, if he wasn't a crybaby, no one would know that he used to be. Nobody here would remember that I had split my pants in front of the senior girls' gym and been humiliated. You got to be who you wanted and could leave behind life's early embarrassments. My father's existence was the first thing that I changed. He became a dead war hero.

After school that first winter, my brothers and I played hockey on the pond behind the school. Quite a few boys liked to play, and we could usually muster up a couple of teams. Peter was not very keen, and he chose to sit out or go home and read comics more often than he played. We didn't have any place to get new comics, and he just read the same ones over and over again.

Paul was very interested in playing hockey, but he wasn't a very good skater. Henri, Alexi, or I would have to do up his skates for him. Nothing would discourage him though, and he insisted on coming along anytime that we went. We often tried to sneak out without him, but he would hear us, or Mama would make us take him along. He liked to drop the puck at the beginning of each play, and usually got under foot when we were playing. His stick was two feet longer than he was, and between trying to skate and holding the stick, he had little time to look where he was going.

In the summer, the pond became a swimming hole. There were a lot of black flies and mosquitoes around the pond, and we went through a lot of calamine lotion.

Mama sent and received letters every week from our sisters. Rachel now had a job in a doctor's office, and Jacquelyn was expecting a baby. George had replaced Tommy, and he was now the *love* of Rachel's life.

In Auburn, there was a general store, a post office, a tavern, a small grocery store, and a café. A delivery truck, driven by the handsome Jakes, came to town twice a week. He brought with him meats, dairy products, and gossip from Fort St. Luke, a town ten miles away. This made it hard for the small grocery store to compete.

M. Trudeau ran the grocery store. As well as not being handsome, he was grumpy and suspicious of everyone . . . especially kids. Because of this, it was a game to see how much penny candy we could steal without getting caught. He seldom caught anyone because we would go in a group. We never went in unless one person had a few cents. No one kid took anything of more value than could be covered by the person with the money. If M. Trudeau caught someone with candy and challenged him, the person with the money would say that he was intending to pay for it. Five or ten cents usually changed hands and seventy-five cents worth of candy would walk out of the door.

4

Robert Drapeau, the lawyer for most of the people in the area, shared an office with the Reeve. M. Drapeau's legal work consisted mainly of real estate deals and some wills. He dealt with some small scrapes that people got themselves into, but he didn't have any big criminal cases.

The police station stood in the middle of the main street. This served an area of a hundred or so square miles, and it employed two policemen. Though the area was big, there were probably no more than five hundred people in the whole district. Seldom was there anyone at the station, because whoever was on duty was usually out in the beat-up, old station wagon that served as a police car. Sometimes it was used as a taxi to take drunks home after a night of revelry.

Mama was happy, and she enjoyed the work she was doing. Maurice was at our house more often than I liked, but so seldom was I home that I tried to ignore him. Mama acquired more furniture for the living room when an old man in town had died, and his only family had no interest in moving his things. Mr. Drapeau told Mama that there would be a big auction sale, but since he was in charge of liquidating the estate assets, he wanted to sell as much of the furniture before hand, in order to save the auction fees. I guess the auctioneer charged a percentage on everything he sold plus mileage.

Mama had an eye for antiques that the lawyer didn't. She got some things very cheaply, and some things that M. Drapeau thought wouldn't sell, Mama got for nothing. Mama brought home enough stuff to fill the gaps in the living room. A wonderful old cherry wood dining table replaced the old kitchen table, which was relegated to the back porch.

She made a lot of friends, and she also was able to leave some of her history behind. She seemed to like the idea of telling people that our father was dead and adopted the story. As far as anyone in town knew, she was a widow. Maurice even went along with the fable, even though he didn't understand the humiliation attached to having someone desert you.

Less than a year after we moved, the logging closed down and most of the townspeople were left unemployed. The tavern did a better business than before, with the unemployed loggers who hadn't moved on to another camp. One of our sources of entertainment had been removed when M. Trudeau was forced to close his store. The population had dropped, and he had barely made a living before with the logging in full swing.

Maurice had gone to work in another camp about one hundred miles away. We didn't see him as much, and I didn't miss him. Mama never said anything, but I got the feeling that she was relieved. Lately, she seemed to lose patience with him when he was around very much. They didn't fight, but she had become so independent, she was not about to let another man run her life.

There had been some warning before the closing of the camp, and Mama had started supplementing her income, waiting on tables at the café, and selling her pies and cakes to the café and tavern. When the camp closed, she got a job at the tavern cooking. There was not a lot of call for food however, and she ended up waiting on the drinkers.

The licensing laws dictated that bars and taverns close between 3:30 p.m. and 7:00 p.m. The happy drinkers didn't usually want to go home after they were just getting that insightful glow that can only be induced by alcohol. They had just begun solving the world's ills and couldn't possibly lose their train of thought by sobering up. My mother found this gap in the market, and she capitalized on it. She started bootlegging. She didn't call it bootlegging, saying that she was just serving people drinks in her house. She preferred to say that she was running a speakeasy.

With her flirtatious and outgoing personality, she quickly built up a clientele of regulars who came to our house after the pub closed in the afternoon and stayed until the pub reopened. Some stayed longer. On Friday and Saturday nights, she would also have people after the nightly closing of the pub at 10:30 p.m. Once she had established regular customers, she found that she could earn a decent living from her speakeasy, so she quit working at the tavern. After that, every night except Sunday and Monday, she would have a house full of patrons. Music would play, and the talk would get louder, making it necessary to turn up the music. Some nights, mostly on weekends, the hi-fi would be cranked right up, and in the summer, we all moved upstairs to the attic to get some sleep.

Mama hadn't anticipated this when she moved in, but seemed glad to have the attic. She hired a couple of her customers to insulate, panel, and hook up the electricity. A couple of space heaters were purchased. The second summer, the attic became the common bedroom for all of us. Alexi and Henri hung blankets to create borders to their spaces. These also blocked out the light when they were up there, and we were supposed to be sleeping.

That same summer Henri started helping Mama, collecting bottles, dumping ashtrays, bringing beer from the basement, and washing glasses. Our refrigerator couldn't store all the ice that was needed to keep the business going, and Mama arranged to buy an old, used freezer from a couple leaving town for greener opportunities. It was discovered that the basement stairs were too steep and narrow to take the freezer so more wiring had to be done in the mudroom to accommodate it.

Mama worked hard, getting up early in the morning to bake her wonderful pies, make our breakfasts and lunches, and get us all off to school. She was always up late at night even when there were no happy sots and drunken philosophers. I often marveled at her bright and cheerful manner.

She didn't drink herself, and she often commented that she didn't like drunks. This seemed odd to me because she did nothing to discourage them, and it appeared that she had a hand in manufacturing them.

My mother was a beautiful woman. This was not only my opinion, but also that of many of the men who frequented our house. She was short with dark hair and brown eyes that sparkled when she laughed and flashed when she was angry. She had her work cut out for her and never seemed to run out of energy. She drank Coke by the gallon, and I guess she ran on pure caffeine. The Coke she had for the drinkers and herself, and it was rarely shared with us.

5

It wasn't hard to slip into the house unseen, with our stash of Coke on the afternoon of our escapades. We were able to change and wash up before supper. The house was full, and the local drunks were keeping Mama busy with their loud demands and noisy talk.

I sometimes would listen from the top of the stairs. They would talk and argue. Their conversations seldom varied. There were only three or four subjects that occupied them, and each would restate their opinion daily. The closing of the logging operation was on top of the list, even though it had happened more than a year ago. All the men would have a different culprit to blame for the closing, from the owner of the operation to the reeve, (if he wasn't present). I was only eleven and didn't know much, but I figured the camp had closed due to lack of customers and lack of profit. I did know that its closure created more money in my mother's pocket, and she never complained of its loss.

Another thing the men talked about, when he wasn't present, was the reeve himself. He seemed to be the cause of all the woes in town, including the disintegration of morals of the younger generation.

The lack of morals would get the men into heated debates as they vented their spleen against all kids, their own included. They could not understand why kids no longer respected their elders and didn't know how to listen. I wondered when they ever saw their kids to know if they were listening or not.

Anyhow, on that night, my brothers and I were upstairs after a wonderful supper of meatloaf and roast potatoes, (crispy on the outside and soft in the middle). Mom sure knew how to cook. Meatloaf was one of my favorites. The sage and onion were balanced in just the right blend. She cut it in slabs, and we covered it with her homemade chili sauce. I still don't know how she managed to have our supper ready ten minutes after everyone was gone.

Peter, Paul, and I were in our room talking and horsing around as we got ready for bed. My two older brothers were in their room supposedly doing their homework.

Mom yelled up the stairs at me to come down. The tone of her voice was less than friendly, and my brothers looked anxious as I opened the door. I went to the top of the stairs and peered down.

"Yes, Mama," I said. I saw her at the foot of the stairs, and I saw that Fern Garceau was standing about three feet away from her. Fern was one of the policemen, and sometimes dogcatcher and truant officer.

"Come down here." She had that angry flashing-eyed look that foretold of storm clouds and loss of privileges and/or additional chores.

I trudged down the stairs with my most confused and innocent expression planted on my face, and looked askance at my mother.

"Yes?" I repeated.

"Where were you and your brothers today?" she asked in a very quiet voice. Mama seldom yelled, and the quiet voice was scarier than a loud one.

I weighed the probability of her already knowing the answer against the odds of lying my way out of trouble, and opted for the lie.

"At school," indignation filled my voice to demonstrate that the thought of me being elsewhere was a preposterous insult.

"Fern here tells me that you, Peter, and Paul were seen coming out of the arena. Don't lie to me." Mama sounded impatient and disappointed. I think I would have preferred yelling.

"But we were at school," I persisted. Once a path was chosen, I had to stick to it.

Fern looked at me and said, "Robin, you and your brothers were seen coming out of the arena, and your teacher says you weren't at school."

There was no point in further denial, and my brothers would confirm these facts in a second. They were impossible with secrets and changed track with any lie they tried ever before properly testing it and seeing how it was greeted.

I hung my head. There was nothing to say, and I couldn't come up with any excuse that would improve the situation.

Fern looked at Mama and shook his head. "I'm sorry, Daphne, but I have to serve these papers to you. You know that if it was up to me, I wouldn't, but too many people think you are given special treatment, and they want justice."

I could see his frustration and embarrassment. Everyone knew he had a soft spot for Mama, but then he wasn't alone.

"What exactly are we talking about, Fern?" She wanted to have the whole picture so she could work her way through it. Mama wasn't one to bury her head in the sand, and with seven kids, she wasn't blind to our faults.

Fern's embarrassment grew, and a red flush crept up his neck and into his cheeks. "They are charged with breaking and entering, vandalism and theft, as well as truancy."

Wow! I didn't recognize myself! I thought we had just played hooky and taken some Coke.

"What!" My mother's voice was no longer quiet. In fact, I had never heard it so loud.

Fern looked at the floor, and Mama snatched the papers from his hand. She read them and sputtered. Fern shuffled his feet, obviously wanting to go and not knowing how to make his exit.

"They have to be in juvenile court in Fort St. Luke on Monday," he muttered.

Mom turned from him to me, not knowing who to yell at. "Oh, get out, Fern!"

He scurried away, and she slammed the door behind him. She then spun around as I was attempting to retreat up the stairs.

"*You*! Get back here. Peter! Paul! Get down here!" she railed.

Paul was whimpering, and Peter had his head down, tears running down his face. Peter caved first, blaming me and Paul for our misconduct, saying that it was Paul's idea to go in and mine to take the pop. He tried to claim innocence. Sometimes, I thought he must have been adopted; he couldn't see that blaming everyone else only made Mama madder and would probably get him beat up real quick (just as soon as she wasn't looking, and I could give him a good thumping!).

"It doesn't matter whose idea it was—you are all in this together! God knows what this will cost me. Go to bed. I don't want to look at any of you." She headed for the phone as we ran up the stairs, knowing that the more she saw of us, the angrier she would get. The best thing in these situations was to become invisible.

Our older brothers were, of course, waiting at the top of the stairs with questions. I told them what we had done, and for once, they had nothing to say.

We could hear Mama on the phone talking to Robert Drapeau. Her voice was hysterical at the beginning, but she calmed down after about fifteen minutes.

At breakfast, she told us that we would probably be fined for damages and would have to pay for the Coke.

"Don't think that it will be me paying for it either!" she snapped. "You will have to work off whatever fine there is. I may pay it initially, but you will work for five cents an hour until you have paid me back. That will mean that you do everything I ask for a long, long time." She stretched the end of the sentence out so that the "long, long time" sounded like several lifetimes.

We didn't know how much it was going to cost in monetary terms, but in time, we were aware that we would probably spend the rest of our lives as slaves. Of course, playing or going anywhere but school would be out of the question.

It was Saturday, and it promised to be a miserable weekend. It was.

We kept a low profile as the direction of Mama's anger moved from us, to the person who had reported us, to the law for treating boyish pranks like a full-blown adult crime.

So the pendulum of her emotions went for the three days that we waited for the trial. Once having been caught, as always, the worst for me was over. All I had to do was wait for my mother to cool, or so I thought.

6

We were slicked, spit, and polished to the point of losing our identities when the dreaded day came. Mama had hired a cab, and we rode into town in solemn silence, afraid to speak. Her nervousness had manifested itself in strange ways in the last few days. We sat, barely breathing in the back of the cab, with my mother in the front seat, staring stonily ahead.

The driver gave up on his attempts to make conversation, and an uncomfortable quiet prevailed. Paul squirmed in the middle and Peter stared out of the window, biting his nails and not even trying to hide his fearful tears. My shirt, one which had been too small the year before, was done up to the top button. I fidgeted with the collar, and I was convinced I would choke to death.

We arrived in front of a large, two-story stone building. Ornate brass handled doors with lions carved into the surface and Latin words inscribed underneath topped the wide steps to the building. These opened into an imposing lobby with a twenty eight-foot ceiling that reached up the two stories of the building.

Around the perimeter of the lobby, but fourteen feet up, there was a railing outlining a balcony. On the inside of the balcony, there were many closed doors. The balcony could be reached by ascending the staircase that stood in the center of the lobby.

A guard was sitting at a desk near the front of the lobby. My mother was about to approach him when Robert entered the building. He nodded at us and walked up to Mama, taking her elbow.

He led us up the stairs to the second floor and opened one of the many doors along the hallway. Oppressive, dark wood prevailed throughout the room, including the huge bench in the front center of the room. A railing with a gate about two-thirds of the way into the room slowed down the approach to the bench. The walls were covered in dark wood. The ceiling was outlined with plaster around the perimeter and punctuated with lions in each corner, and in the center of each wall. A huge light hung in the center of the room. There were no windows. The furniture consisted of dark wooden chairs and a couple of tables beyond the gate. We were directed to sit on the chairs behind the table on the left. The door to the side of the bench opened, and two men entered the room, nodding at our lawyer as they passed.

Mama was whispering to our lawyer, and the two men whispered to each other. The whispers seemed to make the silence deafening instead of breaking it. I remember Uncle Ramon's funeral. The same kind of noisy quiet filled the room. It was like a sauna of silence that made the air hard to breathe, and no matter how much air you inhaled, you couldn't get enough oxygen. I could feel a prickly sweat under my collar, and the more I concentrated on being still, the more I wanted to move. My muscles tensed with the effort to be immobile, and the discomfort was all that I could think about.

Eventually, the door opened again and a tall man with gray hair and black robe, entered the room. I looked at him and realized that I had seen him at our house several times in the late afternoons. As he sat behind the bench, I felt a surge of relief. I assumed we had a friend in the position of authority. I glanced over at my mother and saw her shoulders relax a bit as she watched him sit down. He didn't look at her, but focused his attention on some papers that had been lying on the bench in front of him. He looked up at the two men sitting at the other table.

"We are going to hear the case against the Le Blanc brothers," he announced. "Please read the charges, Mr. Green."

One of the men stood up and said, "The charges are quite minor, my worship, but their situation leads us to believe that these young lads would continue on into a life of crime and amorality if they are not redirected immediately." He paused, and I wondered what *amorality* meant. He looked at my brothers and me, giving us a pitying smile.

"They entered the arena in Auburn unlawfully and stole a case of Coke, leaving a great mess of Coke and paper all over the second floor.

They vandalized the bingo equipment and caused damages in the area of 150 dollars.

How much was 150 dollars divided by five cents? We were doomed.

"My Lord, these three innocent children, mere babies, are brought here not because they are bad children, but because they do not know the difference between right and wrong. They live in a house of ill repute with drunkards and prostitutes present at all hours of the day and night."

At this point, a yelp escaped my mother, and she whispered furiously to our lawyer.

I wasn't sure what he was saying or what his words meant, but the picture he was painting was unrecognizable as our home.

Continuing as if there had been no interruption, he said, "It is our contention that these kids would be better served if they were removed from their mother's home and put in a home of rehabilitation, where they will learn moral values and the teachings of the Lord—a place where they will learn love and decency, and be better prepared for the life that lies ahead."

"I strongly suggest," he continued, "that they be removed to the St. Joseph's Training School for Boys in Parques, Ontario."

The judge looked over his glasses at us and said to our lawyer, "Do you have anything to say that would prevent me from considering these recommendations, M. Drapeau?"

Robert stood up and said, "We do not deny these charges of theft and vandalism, your worship, but the unsubstantiated charges against the boys' mother are slanderous and grossly unfair. The punishment recommended by my colleague is extreme to the limit, like amputating your head to get rid of a cold."

"My client," he continued, "The boys' mother is willing to pay for any damages done to the arena and for the case of Coke taken. She is also willing to pay a fine for their misdeeds, and is willing to have them do community work. You will see that these boys have never been in trouble before and that, for a first offense, of not just juveniles, but children, who haven't even reached puberty, this is a ridiculous proposal."

Mr. Green interrupted, "Do you deny that Mme. Le Blanc sells alcoholic beverages in her home illegally?"

Robert turned to him and smiled, "How can I? You yourself have been a fairly regular customer."

In another situation, and if the object of this joke had not been my mother, I might have found this funny. As it was, no one was laughing. Mr.

Green did get very red however, and the judge quickly interrupted in case it was pointed out that he too, was a faithful customer.

"Mr. Green's morals are not the issue here, and I think that he deserves an apology. I also agree with him in his diagnosis of the situation. The children will be released in the care of the Children's Aid until they can be escorted to Parques," dictated the judge.

"I object," our lawyer jumped to his feet. "The vision created by Mr. Green is tainted and far from the truth. Mme. Le Blanc has managed to feed and clothe five boys on her own. They all have reasonable grades in school. I have here their most recent report cards. They have never been accused of even the slightest misdemeanor before. As you can see with their presence here today, they are well behaved and obedient. To be separated from their mother at the ages they are, would damage these children irrevocably." His frustration appeared to be genuine, but it didn't have any effect on the judge.

"Your objection would normally hold some weight, but I have had Mme. Le Blanc before me for bootlegging in the past," said the Judge. "I agree with Mr. Green wholeheartedly that this is not a house conducive to raising young boys with any respect for the law or the property of others. I am not saying that these boys are bad, but their home environment is a perfect recipe for the creation of criminals. I agree with the recommendations made here today, and the children will now be taken into foster care until they can be transported to Parques, and the St. Joseph Training School for Boys."

"No!" My mother yelled at full volume. In her attempt to stand, she knocked over her chair. It was evident that the decision had been made before we had even gone to the court.

Retrospective memory is so influenced by the present that it is not easy to state accurately how I felt at that time. Fear of the unknown seemed to dominate, and even now as I look back, the fear and horror still predominates although, at the time I had no idea just how intense fear can be. It is shocking how easily one's rights and security can be shattered by the actions of others, and how off-handedly they can alter and destroy the direction of the future.

A woman came from the back of the room. She was wearing a blue suit with a white shirt and a red tie. Her thick ankles sprouted up from her matronly black shoes and headed somewhere north of the bottom of the long skirt, its hem was just a few inches from her shoes. Her hair was brown, short, and frizzy; and she approached us with a smile glued on her face. Paul ran behind Mama, and Peter was at Paul's heels. She extended her hand toward Paul and smiled.

"Come with me young man, I will not hurt you," she said.

Paul screamed, and Peter cowered. I just looked on in amazement, to think that this woman thought she could just walk in and take us away with her. My mother held Paul and put her arm around Peter. Her lawyer said something to her, and she looked at us and at him questioningly. The woman was now attempting to grab Paul by the arm, and she no longer supported her smile.

Mama shouted, "You can't have my children. They are not criminals, and nor am I." Tears ran down her face, and the lawyer was trying to reason with her. She spun around to look at him. "What the hell good are you? You told me that I would have to pay a fine, and the children would have to clean up their mess. Now they are being taken away like common criminals! You are a poor excuse for a lawyer."

Mama then turned her wrath on the Judge and said, "Your court here is a joke, and you are the biggest hypocrite I have ever seen. You sit in judgment of me, when I have had to have you carried home in a state of drunkenness. Yes, you have had me in here charged with bootlegging several times, each time you have given me a ten-dollar fine and a wink and paid me back when you came to my home for a drink."

She charged toward the frizzy-haired woman and snarled, "Get your filthy hands off my child."

Paul had become the object of a tug-of-war contest, and Robert finally grabbed my mother's arm and pried her fingers from Paul's arm. With the release, the woman was off balanced and stumbled against the railing. She straightened herself and took Paul's hand. Paul resisted and pulled but could not free himself.

The men from the other bench now came over, and one turned me by the shoulder, and the other took Peter. We were led outside to a wood-paneled station wagon and tossed unceremoniously into the back seat. Once the door closed and the men moved away, I attempted to open the door, but there were no inside handles.

As I struggled with this problem, our kidnapper jumped in the front seat with more agility than one would have expected, and the driver's door opened and a man, whom I had not seen before, got in and started the car. Neither of them acknowledged our existence until our journey ended in front of a large, two-story house. Our doors were opened, and the woman took Paul by the arm, firmly holding it at the elbow, and the man roughly grabbed Peter and me by the upper arms. I squirmed to free myself, but this only made his grip firmer.

"It's not so bad, you know, boys." His voice was friendly, and there was no hostility in his manner. "Some nice people live here, and you will stay here for a day or two. I hope you will behave for them. They are just here to help kids like you. They don't mean you any harm, nor do we.

I didn't believe a word he said, but his pacifying voice seemed to placate Peter, and he calmed visibly.

We went up the steps of the front porch and a beautiful young woman opened the door. She had long, wavy, red hair that framed her face like a mane. She was wearing a bright yellow and white frilly apron over a blue house dress. She smiled at us and opened the door. Her eyes were as blue as the sky, and a dimple appeared on her left cheek when she smiled. A little blond girl, about three years old, clung to her skirt.

"You are just in time. I am making a batch of cookies. I'm about to put the second sheet into the oven. They will be done in less than fifteen minutes." She squatted down in front of Paul and smiled, "I bet you're Paul."

Paul looked up at her pretty, smiling face and nodded. She put out her hand to him, and he took it without any hesitation.

She then looked at Peter and me and said, "I'm Crystal Barney, you can call me Crystal. You will have to tell me, which of you is Peter and who is Robin?" She stood up still holding Paul's hand and led us into the house. The little girl was still hanging onto her dress was sucking her thumb.

Crystal looked down at the child and said to us, "This is Mary. She is a bit shy when you first meet her, but she will talk your ears off when she knows you."

Crystal walked down the hall, and we followed; the people from the car were forgotten. We walked into a toy-strewn living room and through a dining room and into a den. The room was cluttered and full of overstuffed furniture. Sitting on one of the two large couches were three kids—two boys and a girl—they were staring at the most unusual piece of furniture in the room. A television! I knew what television was, but I didn't know anyone who had one. I stared at the screen while live people were riding horses and shooting at each other. I was mesmerized.

Crystal said, "Kids, these are the Le Blanc boys." The girl and two boys turned their heads and waved. They immediately refocused on the television.

Crystal shrugged, "The television seems to cut down on the amount of conversation that goes on in this house. Julie," she pointed to the girl on the couch. "Mark and Pierre, these are Robin, Peter and Paul."

When she said Paul's name, he looked up at her, and she smiled that sunny smile. Paul's face seemed to reflect the glow, and his heart was won. He wasn't the only one.

"I'm going back to the kitchen," she nodded toward a door at the end of the room. "You can stay in here or come out and give me a hand licking the bowl."

Paul didn't let go of her hand, and she moved to the door, little Mary now trying to take Paul's hand out of Crystal's, but Paul was not about to relinquish it. Crystal gave her other hand to Mary as she opened the door and let the smell of cookies waft into the room.

Peter was already sitting in a chair, glued to the television. If Crystal had not been so beautiful, and the smell of cookies not been so tempting, the television would have won my attention, hands down. However, I did think that I would look silly going into the kitchen with the babies, so I stayed in the den wishing I was in the kitchen.

There was no need to try to make conversation with the other kids, so I found a seat and began to watch the amazing machine. The kitchen door opened a little while later, and Crystal was carrying a plate of cookies. Paul was already stuffing one in his face, and Mary was once again clinging to the skirt and scowling at Paul.

"I don't suppose any of you would like some cookies?" She laughed as we all pounced on the plate. "I'll get you some milk, try to keep the crumbs on the coffee table, and not to spill your milk." She went through the door, Mary still in tow.

Paul stayed in the television room this time, grabbing another cookie before he had finished the one in his mouth. He sat on the floor at my feet and stared at the television.

"How do those people all fit in there, Robin?" he asked.

"They aren't really in there," I said. I didn't know where they were or how it was done, but I was really hoping that he wouldn't ask me any more questions that I couldn't answer in front of these new kids.

"Electronic signals are sent through the wires, and the signals turn into pictures and sounds when they reach the television," this came from Pierre, or was it Mark?

"Shhh," hissed Julie. I silently thanked her because I didn't want to get involved in a discussion that would only make me look stupid. We engrossed ourselves in the television until Crystal came in and told us we had to wash up for supper.

"Aw," moaned everyone as she turned off the television. We followed the other kids into the bathroom that was off the kitchen. Crystal poked her nose in the door and said to me, "Your pajamas and clothes have arrived, and I will put them up in your room after supper."

We went into a big kitchen and sat at a table even larger than the one we had at home. There was a man sitting at the head of the table, and he seemed to have taken over Mary's affections. She crawled up on his knee, and he introduced himself.

"I'm John Barney, and you boys will have to tell me your names," he said.

Peter and Paul sat on either side of me, and when they didn't speak up, I said, "I'm Robin, this is Peter and this is Paul."

John and Crystal smiled at each other across the table, and I felt a twinge of something unidentifiable.

"I guess I should tell you something about us, and then you can tell me something about yourselves," John said this while scanning my brothers and me.

"Crystal and I love children, and it seems that we can't have any of our own. We have children stay with us when there is a need," he looked down and smiled at little Mary as he picked her up from his lap and sat her on the chair next to him. The chair had a big book on it to allow her to see over the edge of the table.

He looked at Paul and said, "Would you like a book too, young man?"

Paul, whose nose was resting on the edge of the table, just stared at him. John got up and left the room, returning a minute later with a large atlas. He pulled out the chair, and Paul stood up. After putting the book on the chair, he lifted Paul up on the elevated seat. Paul didn't say a word.

When he sat down again, John continued, "Mary has been with us for six months, and we are hoping that we will be able to adopt her."

Peter piped up, "Where is her mother?"

Crystal jumped in, "Her mother has gone to heaven, and can't look after Mary any more."

I kicked Peter under the table.

"Ow, what did you do that for?" he said. I glowered at him, and he shut up.

I didn't think that anyone could cook as well as my mother, but Crystal had made macaroni and cheese, hotdogs and French fries. For dessert, she served apple crumble drenched with a butterscotch sauce. We ate as though we hadn't eaten for a week. There was a huge blue-and-white-striped milk pitcher in the center of the table. The milk tasted sweet, and we all had seconds.

John told us that there was a barn out back with two dairy cows. The milk was fresh every day, and yes, we could look at them tomorrow. Along with the cows, there were six chickens, two ducks, and a barn cat.

Pierre, Julie, and Mark went to school the next day, but we stayed with Crystal, not having to return to our school. It turned out that Julie and Mark were brother and sister, and Pierre was an orphan. Pierre had never known any parents, and had been moved from foster home to foster home since he was a baby. All that was said about Julie and Mark was that their parents were unable to look after them at this time.

We went out to the barn with John in the morning, and he taught us how to milk the cows. Peter had no liking for this, and after the first morning, he stayed in the house. Paul made valiant efforts to milk the cows, but when he sat on the stool and tried to lean into the cow, his head was too low, and the teats hung down in his eyes. What a funny sight he was. We laughed, and with our laughter, Paul kept putting his head under the cow's sack so that her teats hung around his head like a limp, upside-down crown.

John finally put Paul on his lap so that he could reach the udders. It was a while before he managed to extract any milk, and the cow didn't seem too happy about giving it to him. John said that I was a natural, and I managed to collect a whole bucket.

It seemed that John did a lot of things. He was a tinsmith, a carpenter, and a mechanic. He had a workshop built on the side of the barn. I spent most of my time watching John do his work. He was fixing a motor, and making some eave's troughs for a neighbor. I would hand him things as he needed them, and I found myself telling him about our life, even telling him about my father's desertion. I talked about our mother and our life, and told him of our crimes. He didn't pry, but I felt a need to tell him things, things I couldn't tell anyone else. Through the process of telling him everything, I began to look at things a little differently. He didn't tell me that I was bad, and he laughed about the arena, seeming to understand the compulsion to go in and explore. He led my conversation without saying anything. When I told him about the court, he just shook his head and looked disgusted.

"Hand me the snips, Robin," was all he said.

I liked him. He was the first adult male I had ever trusted or liked very much. I didn't even resent him for being Crystal's husband. It seemed that they belonged together and that one would be a little less without the other. During that week, I didn't even think about home, and I didn't look ahead to our intended destination. Somewhere in the back of my mind, I must have hoped that we would be forgotten with John and Crystal.

Mary had decided that Paul was her friend after the first night, and she relinquished Crystal's skirts to follow Paul around the house. When John and I came into the house, she left Paul and followed me around.

"Robin?" she would say.

"Yes," I would answer.

"Nuttin." She would smile and say again, "Robin?"

After three or four times, I would laugh, and Crystal would smile dotingly at the child. She was loved by all except Peter, who didn't like her talking. He spent his whole time in front of the television lost to the world. He had become addicted and even resented being interrupted for meals.

On Saturday night after supper, we were cleaned up and taken to Mass in Fort St. Luke. We hadn't been to Mass since we moved up north. My mother had rosary beads, icons, and pictures of Jesus all over, and she said her *Ave Maria* regularly, but she never seemed to have time or the inclination to go to church. This was no hardship for me or my brothers. We all preferred to be outside, without the confinements of church. We didn't complain though, when John and Crystal informed us of our destination; it was unthinkable to do anything than to follow their wishes. They seemed to create a desire to please.

Sunday morning, John and Crystal looked upset. I thought they had quarreled and didn't ask questions. We ate breakfast, and when Crystal stood up to clear up, John pushed away from the table. I got up and followed him into the barn. Paul jumped up and said, "Will you help me put on my boots, Robin?"

"Not today, Paul," John said, "I want to go alone with Robin to the barn." My heart sank, and I wondered what I had done wrong. I pulled my galoshes over my shoes, dawdling over the buckle, feeling a remorse for having upset them, even though I didn't know what I had done.

We went into the barn, and John pulled out the two stools, and placed one in front of each cow. He indicated the stool I was to take, and he sat on the other. He blew into his hands, warming them and began to milk. I followed his lead and waited. I leaned my head into the cow's side and John spoke.

"We received a phone call this morning, Robin." I looked at his face and saw him fighting back tears. "I don't know how to say this easy, so I will just say it."

My stomach curdled my breakfast, and I wanted him to stop speaking. Wishing doesn't make it so, and he once again found his voice.

"Tomorrow morning, you and your brothers will be going to the school in Parques. I will take you to the train station, and a man will meet you there and escort you to the school."

I turned my head and buried it in the cow's side, trying to hide my tears. I shook with grief. The cow let out a bellow of objection, and I felt John's hand on my shoulder.

I couldn't stop crying, and John turned me around. I buried my face in his stomach and cried. He did nothing to stop me; he just put his hand on my head and let me soak up his calm.

When my tears were finally spent, I sniffed. John reached in his pocket and pulled out a freshly pressed hanky and handed it to me. I blew my nose loudly, and we both laughed, glad of the distraction.

"I can't tell you how sad this makes me, Robin," he said. "In this past week, Crystal and I have gotten to know you, and we realize that you are just three ordinary kids."

He thought about this for a moment and said, "No, not ordinary, exceptional. You are not hooligans as we were led to believe. You are polite and well behaved. You are not dead, however, and I don't understand how the court could expect you to be anything but the curious boys you are. It makes me angry, and I feel frustrated and unable to do anything." His voice was shaking in anger and tears of frustration ran down his face. "I would give anything to have a son like you."

Why did he have to say that? I could feel the tears once again in my eyes, and my throat swelled with a lump that I couldn't swallow. I turned away, and my need to make him feel better was greater than my self-pity.

"We'll be okay, just you wait and see. My Mama's lawyer will get us out. Just you wait."

"Do you want to tell your brothers? I thought that I would ask you first." His head was bowed as if he was ashamed of himself.

I straightened myself up and said, "I can tell Peter all right, but I think it will be hard to tell Paul. He seems to have moved right in. He's just a baby and doesn't understand."

"I think that maybe Crystal should tell Paul," John said. "She seems to have the magic of making things okay. She isn't clumsy with words, like I am."

I agreed, not wanting the task, knowing that I had just learned one of life's lessons about being male. Anything unsavory could be avoided, if we admitted that we were unqualified. In these cases, we could allow the women to be superior to us.

We walked back to the house and in through the kitchen. John had managed to get the cows to donate half a bucket of milk, and I had failed totally. He set the bucket on the floor and nodding at it, said to Crystal, "We'll have to try again later. Daisy and Tulip didn't want to cooperate."

Crystal, her hands immersed in dishwater, nodded and smiled sadly. She wiped her hands on her apron and came over to me. She put her hand under my chin and looked into my face. "We have to be brave and believe that there is some good that will come out of this."

She pulled me to her, rocked me, and bending down she kissed the top of my head. I don't know where all the tears came from, but I seemed to have produced a new crop. This crying was exhausting.

Mary and Paul could be heard coming in from the television room. I quickly pulled away, embarrassed and ashamed of my weakness.

"Mine," whined Mary.

Paul was carrying Mary's teddy bear, and Mary was trying unsuccessfully to grab it.

Crystal moved away from me, and I fled into the bathroom.

I could hear John trying to reason with Mary and Paul. Paul finally said, "Okay, you big baby, you can have it back."

I washed my face and blew my nose and reentered the kitchen. Crystal was emptying the sink and John suggested to Mary that they go upstairs and find her sweater.

Crystal said to me, "Robin, why don't you have a talk with Peter? Paul and I will do some serious coloring."

Paul liked this idea and couldn't believe his luck at having Crystal all to himself. I went into the television room and there was Peter sitting in front of the television, oblivious to everyone and everything. Julie and Pierre were sitting on the couch, and Mark was playing with a truck on the floor.

"Peter," I said.

"Shhh, I'm watching this," he said not looking away from the television.

"Peter, I have to talk to you," I insisted.

"Not now. After this show." He still hadn't taken his eyes off the screen.

I stood in front of the screen and said, "Now!"

"Hey!" yelled all four.

Peter finally looked at me and realized that I wasn't going to take no for an answer. "Okay, what do you want to talk about?"

"Not here," I said, "In our room."

"Can't you just tell me here," he whined.

"No," I said no more and headed for the door.

I turned as I passed through the dining room and saw Peter looking back at the television screen. I walked back to him and grabbed his arm and pulled.

"I'm coming," he said sulkily, "You don't have to grab me."

I finally got him to our room and pushed him down on the bed. A lot of my anger wasn't with Peter, but the situation.

"Now listen to me. This is important," I said.

He picked up a comic book from the floor and opened it. I slapped it out of his hand and said, "Will you *please* pay attention!"

"I'm listening! What makes you think you can boss me around?" he yelled.

"I'm not trying to boss you around, but I have to tell you something important." I didn't know how Peter felt, or if he felt anything, so I didn't know how to tell him. It must have been really hard on John and Crystal having to tell me and Paul.

Peter just looked at me. Fear started to appear in his eyes, and he said, "We have to go to that school, don't we?"

"Yes," I said.

"Oh god," he moaned. "It is so good here. I was hoping that they had forgotten about us and that we would be allowed to stay here forever."

"You knew better than that," I ridiculed him for having the same pipe dream as mine. I softened as I saw the tears running down his face. I don't think that more tears had been shed in our whole family as had been in this last week. I knew that when we went back downstairs, we would find Paul in the same shape.

"Stop crying," I said roughly, clearing my throat and forcing myself to be brave.

Paul sniffed and wiped his nose on his sleeve. "I might as well go back and watch television When do we have to go?"

"Tomorrow morning," I said.

That was all he wanted to know, and he returned to the television. I met John and Mary in the hall, Mary was now wearing a bright red cardigan over her pink overalls. She looked at me and said, "Robin?"

I took a deep breath and said gruffly, "What?"

"Robin?" she repeated.

John picked her up and tickled her, "You little monkey."

Mary wasn't to be distracted though, and she reached down to me and put her hand on my cheek. "Robin?" her eyebrows were raised in a giant question mark.

That was all it took. I fled back into the temporary sanctuary of our bedroom and threw myself down on the bed. How could it hurt so much? This was more painful than the day we were in the courthouse. What had these people done to us?

I knew that I had to put on a brave face. I didn't want Peter or Crystal to know what a baby I was. It didn't seem so bad that John should know though.

I finally pulled myself together and went back to the kitchen. Crystal had Paul on her knee. His head was buried in her shoulder, and she was rocking him and making soothing noises. Little Mary was tugging at Paul's sleeve saying, "Pauli?"

I walked over to the sink and got myself a glass of water and saw that John was again pulling on his boots.

"I guess I had better give Daisy and Tulip another chance to give us some milk." He said this seeming to think that some explanation was needed for his exit. I nodded and almost fell over Mary as I turned.

"Robin?" I looked down at her and forced myself to laugh. Poor little kid. She didn't know what was going on, but she knew there was something wrong.

I picked her up and twirled her around. "Come on, Mary. Let's see where your teddy bear has gone." We went into the television room and found it on the floor. Mary picked it up and headed back into the kitchen. She walked over to Paul and pulled his arm.

"Here, Pauli," she said, holding the teddy bear out to him.

Paul turned and sniffed. He reached down and took the bear, held it to his chest and snuggled back into Crystal's arms.

I didn't feel like watching television, and I didn't know what to do with myself. "I think I'll go back to the barn and help John," I said to Crystal.

She nodded and smiled. I put on my boots and coat and wandered outside. The thought of running away occurred to me, but I didn't know where to go. Maybe the school wouldn't be so bad. After all, we thought this place would be awful, and it turned out to be the most wonderful place I had ever been. Not that our house had been a bad place, and I missed Mama a lot, but she wasn't there for us like John and Crystal. She had to earn a living to support us and that took up most of her time.

John was now successfully milking Tulip, and I sat on the other stool. We sat in silence for a while and then John seemed to read my thoughts.

"Maybe it won't be so bad," he said. "One other time, we had a boy come to us for a while before he was sent to that school. He wrote to us and said he was playing hockey and swimming in the summer. I guess there is a pool there, and they have a big recreation room with pool tables and a television. They make maple syrup there and have farm animals. It can't be too bad, or the Catholic Church wouldn't run it."

I didn't know whom he was trying to convince, but I was glad for the information. My only impression of the school was that it was a place of punishment, kind of like a jail for kids. Nobody had told me anything about the school, and I had never heard of it until last week. The way John described it, it sounded kind of neat.

"Do you really think that it will be okay?" I asked, trusting him to tell me the truth.

"On the surface, it sounds all right, and I haven't heard anything to the contrary. It is just that you boys are all so young to be away from your home!" he ended in frustration.

When he had finished milking, we didn't go back into the house right away. John wandered into his workshop and started puttering around. Neither of us said anything for a long time, both lost in our own thoughts.

Finally, John said, "The more I think about it, the more I realize that this school must be an all-right place. It's not just for kids who have done something wrong, some of the boys there are orphans, and they haven't found adoptive parents. The church looks after children, and really, I have heard first-hand of the fine sports and activities they have there. Maybe it will be like going to summer camp—only for longer.

I thought for a while and realized that I didn't even know how long we were supposed to be at the school. I asked John if he knew, and he said he hadn't heard anything about that.

I fantasized about playing hockey and baseball all the time. I loved sports. I didn't mind school and was fairly good at math, but I found physical activities more alluring. Up until now, I had some idea that there would be bars on the windows, and we would be locked in cells. This new perception of the school was a great improvement, and it eased the pain of leaving John and Crystal. Of all my wishes though, I had secretly harbored the dream of having them adopt us, as well as Mary. With this thought, I felt disloyal to Mama.

We finally went in the house for lunch. Pierre and Mark were already at the table horsing around. They looked up when we came in, and Mark ran over to John, who gave him a friendly jab in the shoulder and said, "How's it going, big guy?"

Mark grinned and said, "Okay. John, do you think you can help me with my science project?"

"Sure," said John. "Where are Julie and Peter?"

"Where else? In the television room glued to that box," informed Pierre.

Julie was as addicted to the television as Peter. Maybe it was a way to escape unpleasant situations, but in Peter's case, I knew it was a way to avoid living. He did the same with his comic books.

When we all sat down to lunch, John announced that we would be going the next day to the school. The picture he created of the school was positive, and I was even convinced that we would be all right. He told of the fine opportunity that we were being offered. The school was like a private boarding school with a pool and hockey rinks, baseball and football fields, farm animals, a maple syrup bus, a gym, pool tables, television, and great teachers. Peter perked up at the mention of television, and when John had finished, Mark and Pierre looked envious.

Paul was not to be lured so easily, however. He needed parents, at least one parent, and he could not be offered anything that was worth more to him than the comfort of an adult's lap. He watched Peter and me very carefully to gauge our reactions, and he tried to reflect what he saw. He decided that if we were all right with it, that the school might not be so awful after all, and that it might be a kind of adventure.

That night, when we were all in bed, with the lights out, Paul whispered, "Robin? Are you awake?"

"Yes, Paul, I'm awake," I whispered back.

"It might be all right like John says," he said, "But if you had your choice, where would you rather be?" Paul wanted some straight answers.

There was no way I was going to admit my disloyalty to Mama by admitting that I would like to stay right there, where we were, so I said, "At home, of course."

"I'd rather stay right here with Crystal and John. Is that bad? I like it here. I like not having noisy men in our house every day. I like coloring with Crystal and going to the barn with John and not being the youngest, and I like the way Crystal's hair smells, like sunshine, and she listens to me and not just saying 'yes, yes, yes' when I want to tell her something."

He started to cry a bit, "Is it bad that I want to stay here instead of going home?"

Peter snorted, "What difference does it make? We are going to the school tomorrow, and that's that. No sense in dreaming about being here or with the man in the moon." I couldn't tell from his tone if he was happy or sad or if he cared where he was. It seemed that he was uninfluenced by others, almost as if the world went on around him, and he had some kind of barrier against it.

I lay awake for a long time that night and heard Crystal and John come up the stairs. Their voices could be heard through the wall, and I thought I heard her crying. John was making comforting noises, and eventually, the house was quiet. I got up and stood at the window. The sky was clear, and the moon was in its first half. Fresh snow was falling, and the trees gathered a heavy coat of snow, making things seem closer. The trees seemed to be embracing the area around the house, trying to protect it from the outside.

I must have slept. I woke to find Mary standing beside my bed, "Robin?" She had her teddy bear in one arm and her thumb in her mouth. I was going to miss her. I sure hoped that Crystal and John would be able to keep her. She deserved to have a good family. I gave her my bravest smile and said, "What are you doing up so early?"

"Baffoom," she said as she proceeded to climb up on my bed. My brothers were asleep, and the house was in darkness. Only the light from the upstairs bathroom was on. I moved over so that she could crawl in, and she squirmed to make herself comfortable, pulling my blankets from me. Once she had burrowed her way in, she put her hand on my cheek and said, "Robin." Closing her eyes, she immediately fell asleep.

The next thing I heard was Crystal admonishing Mary for stealing my covers and taking over my bed. Mary sat up, smiled, and said, "Robin," as she pointed at me.

"That's okay," I said, "I am going to miss her."

Crystal frowned and bit her lip. She turned to leave and said, "You leave early, but I think that you could sleep for another twenty minutes or so."

I lay there after she left and stared at the ceiling, wanting life to halt in this house. Regretting my very existence, I blinked back some more tears, cursing myself for being a baby. I was going to have to get tough. I vowed then and there that I wouldn't let anyone get this close to me again.

Paul awoke and stumbled out of bed to the bathroom. He came back in and asked if he had heard voices. I explained about Mary and Crystal. He just nodded and started to put on his clothes. I resigned myself to getting up, and once I was dressed, nudged Peter, saying, "Come on, lazy bones, we have to get up now."

He groaned and pulled the covers over his head. I went downstairs to the kitchen. Crystal already had the coffee percolating, and Mary was standing on a chair next to her, helping her mix pancake batter. Crystal's hair was a mass of curls that formed a red halo around her face. Her face was still full of sleep, and she looked as childlike as Mary. What a pretty sight they both were.

I stood looking out of the window. The new snow made you realize the number of animals and birds that passed through the yard. The tracks of deer and dogs, squirrels and rabbits, birds and raccoons had left the virgin snow trampled. There were a couple of jays on the feeding table, and a squirrel hanging upside down, trying to break into the feeder. I enjoyed the peaceful view, knowing that in a few hours my life would be anything but peaceful, but not knowing how it would be changed.

Breakfast was quiet. Crystal had made a special treat of pancakes and sausages, and Mary wanted to pour the milk. She did this with a lot of help from John. We had an awkward good-bye scene with Pierre, Mark, and Julie, and a heartbreaking farewell with Mary and Crystal.

7

John drove us to the train station where Mama and our older brothers, Alexi and Henri, were waiting. John introduced himself to my mother. "Mme. Le Blanc, you have three wonderful boys. I hope that they do will at their new school and that you will be reunited shortly."

This sent Mama into a fit of tears and everyone started to cry.

"I am going to get them back real soon," Mama said, and she stuck out her chin. "They should never have been sent away from me in the first place."

John looked uncomfortable and said, "If there is anything that I can do to help, I would gladly do it."

Mama looked up through her tears, hesitated, and then said, "Maybe you could write to the judge and tell him what good boys they are. Tell him that they are not, and never will be criminals, that I have done a good job raising them. Tell him that they don't need to be taken from their home."

"I can and will do that," John nodded, "And I will get my wife, Crystal, to write as well. They were model children at our house and never gave us a moment of trouble. That of course couldn't happen without proper training before they got there."

"Of course they had proper training!" exclaimed Mama. "They are good boys, and I have taught them to be good boys. They may get up to some childish pranks once in a while, but what child doesn't? They didn't mean any harm." Mama wiped her tears, and you could see that she was starting to get mad all over again at the situation.

As this conversation was taking place, a short rotund man approached. Looking at my mother, he took off his hat and displayed a fringe of brown hair topped with a shiny pate.

"I'm Arthur," he stuttered. "I will be your boys' escort and guardian on the trip to Parques."

"Well, you will just have to turn around and bring them back," snapped my mother. "I will have them released from that school before you even get there!" Her anger was rolling to a full boil.

I was not good at determining ages of people over twenty, but Arthur seemed to be a little younger than Mama. He sported a mustache that seemed to consist of many different colors. Arthur was a social worker who thought he was aiding our welfare and serving on the side of the angels. Mama's yelling at him seemed to make him uncomfortable and gave us permission to show as much resistance as we could.

As Mama stood hollering at Arthur, Fern, our friendly gendarme, was standing at her side. It seemed that the whole town was there to see us off.

"Is there a problem, Daphne?" he asked quite innocently, but was braced for trouble.

"Problem?" she shrieked. "Problem? What gives you that idea, you silly nit? I am the happiest woman in the world today! Every mother wants to rid herself of her babes! Why should I have a problem?" She seethed and hissed like a snake.

Although Fern seemed to shrink, he firmly held his ground. "Now, Daphne, I know you are upset, but this will not be a bad thing. I have known lots of kids who have gone to this school and come out the better for it. Give it a chance. It isn't as if it is forever."

"Can you tell me, smart boy, how long is it for? Nobody has been able to tell me that." She was spitting mad, and Arthur had returned his hat to his head and burrowed into the collar of his gray coat, like a turtle retreating into its shell.

There were a lot more of angry, frustrated words from my mother as she vented at the world and felt powerless to change the situation. The more Fern tried to calm her, the more fuel he added to the inferno.

John shifted his weight from one foot to the other, and he said, "I guess I had better get back, I have chores to do."

Mama looked at him as if she had forgotten him and said, "Please remember to write that letter. We need all the help we can get."

John gave me a manly jab in the jaw, ruffled Peter's hair, and hugged Paul. "Be good, you guys. Crystal and I have the address, and we will write. I hope you will write back."

Finally, Fern and Arthur led us to the train, and Fern held out his arm as a barrier to prevent Mama from snatching us back.

Through my tears, I promised my mother that I would look after my brothers, and Mama promised that we would be home in no time. I figured that she would fix it; she managed to pull off bigger miracles than this. So as the three of us boarded the train. There was a sense of adventure mixed with the fear that there was a slight chance that Mama couldn't fix it; fear also of the unknown—not fear of Arthur. Poor Arthur.

8

Through the window of the train, we watched the rugged scenery flash by for the two hours it took to reach Chambers. There Arthur instructed us to sit tight and stay on the train, telling us that he had to make a phone call to arrange for our bus trip from the train to Parques.

When Arthur had disappeared from sight, I took my two brothers by the hands and led them down to the stairs of the next car. We stood there until we heard the conductor yell, "All aboard!" and saw Arthur mount the steps into our car. We disembarked while he was boarding, and the train started to move.

We waved as we saw Arthur's face pressed against the window, looking at us in ashen despair. Poor Arthur.

I went to the phone booth and asked the operator to call my mother.

"Mom, we have changed our minds and want to come home," I said when I finally got through to her. "We are in Chambers."

Mom was full of questions, but I finally convinced her that we were all alone in Chambers and that she had better come and get us.

She managed to get a friend to drive her to pick us up, and she arrived about two and a half hours later.

On the way home, she told us we would have to go back. Much as she wanted us home she said, she knew that we couldn't just decide on our own to quit the journey. The police would probably have been informed by now that we were missing and would come and get us. When we got home, my brother told Mom that Fern had called to say that Arthur was coming to get us, and that when we arrived home, we were to stay there until Arthur arrived.

Arthur arrived soaked to the bone, very upset and disheveled. He was not very happy, and he had taken a cab 118 miles to retrieve us. By then, Fern was at our house, and it was decided that we would have to stay in the custody of Children's Aide until morning when we could restart our journey.

In the morning, we were back at the train station, and when the train stopped in Chambers, Arthur didn't take his eyes off of us. He wasn't going to be fooled again by our outward youthful innocence.

It was time for breakfast, and we went to the dining car with Arthur. We all decided that hotdogs and French fries would be a fitting meal. Arthur wasn't inclined to agree and suggested toast and cereal. We stubbornly crossed our arms and dug in our heels.

"No," we cried in unison.

Arthur scowled, and seeing it had no influence on us, he added, "Please?"

"No."

Arthur finally saw it our way, and we ate our breakfast in angelic peace.

We had all had an exhausting twenty-four hours and went back to our seats. Paul fell asleep, Peter fell asleep, and I pretended to fall asleep until Arthur had dozed off.

Arthur found us about half an hour later in the baggage car talking to some rail workers who thought that we were nice little boys. Arthur was near the end of his tether. His face had adopted a purple tinge, his eyes seemed to be too big for his sockets, and his mustache stood straight out from his upper lip. He sputtered and ranted and returned us to our seats.

Arthur, like my mother, seemed to think I was incorrigible and did not take his eyes off of me until it was time for dinner.

We disagreed again on the proper diet for the appointed meal. We wanted large bags of chips with Coke. Arthur was determined to show his authority and tried to insist. Again, we had a battle of wills.

After our chips and Coke, I got the distinct feeling that Arthur had developed a strong dislike for me and did not want to adopt me and take him home as his own.

Once we were respectably in our seats, Paul announced that he had to go to the bathroom.

Arthur interpreted this as a request for permission and told Paul that this would be okay. He pointed the way to the washroom.

"I need *you* to take me to the bathroom. I need *you* to help me with my pants," Paul informed him.

Arthur was nonplussed. He gave me a look of accusation and said, "Your brother is seven years old, can't he go to the bathroom on his own?"

"Not when he is scared like this," I responded. "I could go with him if you like."

Arthur looked suspiciously at me and decided that he would take Paul to the bathroom.

"I'm done!" yelled Paul through the door. "Come and wipe my bum."

Arthur was aghast, "You've got to be kidding."

"I won't come out 'till you do," Paul yelled through the door.

I hadn't known just how smart Paul was until then.

Arthur looked at me and said, "Don't you *move.*"

I smiled angelically.

An hour later, Arthur found Peter and me in the mail car. Poor Arthur.

Arthur decided, in order to gain some control, he would order our supper for us. He requested and received four roast beef dinners. We decided to fast.

After our hotdogs and fries, we returned to our seats. The windows were cold and black, and we looked out to find our own reflections looking back. Paul was running out of steam. "I'm tired," he announced, eyes drooping, head unsteady on his scrawny neck.

Sleeping berths had been booked, and Arthur took us to them. I think he was as tired as Paul. Paul was put in the bottom berth across from Arthur. Peter and I were in the top of either bunk. We were ordered to take our clothes off and were left in our underwear. Henry put our clothes in the bottom with Paul. The ladders were taken away to ensure that we did not escape. Poor Arthur.

Arthur was on the bottom berth opposite me. Arthur snored. Once it was clear that he was asleep, Peter and I jumped down from our berths and put our clothes back on. We explored the train from one end to the other, finding it pretty dull because all of the passengers seemed to be sleeping and there wasn't much to do. Most of the lights had been turned down, with just dim lights along the aisles at the floor level on the seats.

The train stopped and did some shunting when we were near the front. We stumbled in between the first and second cars and looked out of the window on one of the doors. We were in a fairly large station.

"What do you think they are doing?" Peter asked while peering out of a window.

"Just shunting, I guess. Maybe they are adding another car." I wasn't that curious; the train had done some of this kind of thing in a couple of other towns. It wasn't long before we started moving again.

"I'm tired," yawned Peter. "I think we should go back and get some sleep."

I had to agree with him. I could barely see straight. I was too tired to resist anymore for the day.

We headed to the back of the train toward our sleeping car. We went through two cars and the first sleeping car. (Ours was the second.) We opened the door at the back of that car to find that we were staring at the caboose. Our sleeping berths, along with the car that contained them were gone! We looked at each other and Peter said, "Did we already go through two sleeping cars?"

"I don't think so but we must have," I said. I turned around to go back. We looked in all the berths, only to find Paul and Arthur were not on this car. We went back through the doors in to a regular coach car. Where had it gone? I spotted the conductor half asleep in one of the seats in the back.

"Excuse me," I said to him.

He snorted and straightened up. "What is it, young fellas? You should be asleep."

"That's what we were trying to do, but we can't find our berths," I said.

"The sleeping car is the next one back," he pointed through the door.

"I know there is one there," I explained, trying to be calm, "But we were in the second sleeping car, and my brother and I went to the bathroom, and a little walk, and when we came back, the second car was gone."

The light seemed to dawn in his eyes, and he groaned, "Oh no. How long were you gone for a walk?"

I didn't really know. It didn't seem like a long time. "Maybe a few minutes, I don't know," I said.

He stood up and straightened his tie. "We just came out of North Bay. There we unhooked the second sleeping car. It was then hooked on to the train going farther east, to Ottawa. This train is now heading south to Toronto. Are your parents on the other train now?"

"Not our parents, but our little brother and a traveling guardian are on the other train."

Peter started to cry, and I was too tired to join him.

The conductor sat us down in the seat he had just vacated. "Stay right here, I will go and talk to the engineer, and radio the other train." He headed off toward the front of the train.

Peter and I sat there feeling more lost than ever. There was a couple in the seat in front of us. They had been sleeping, but the woman turned and looked around the seat. "What are you kids doing making all that racked?" she grumbled, but not really angry, just blurry-eyed.

"Our sleeping car had disappeared and our little brother is on it. We're lost from our train," I sniffed, realizing that I had done a lot of crying in the last couple of days.

"Oh, my goodness," she sat up and nudged her husband. "George, wake up." There were groans coming from the other seat as George tried to ignore his wife.

"George, wake up!" she persisted.

"What," he whined. "I finally got to sleep, and you have to wake me up."

"George, these kids have lost the train they were on," she explained.

"How the heck could they lose the train they were on? They are on the train. If they started out on the train, and they are still on the train, just like us," he said with mock patience, "They haven't lost the train."

His wife explained, "I didn't have the energy to explain it all over again."

"That is too bad dear," said George, his head appeared over the back of the seat, "This is a real problem, boys, but I think you should tell the conductor. There is nothing I can do."

"George! They have all ready told the conductor, I was expecting you to have a little more compassion than that," his wife said this as if he had just failed her in some great way.

"Well, I admit that it *is* a problem, but really, there isn't anything that I can do. What would you have me do anyway?" he grumbled.

"I wouldn't *have* you do anything," retorted his wife in resignation. "I just thought you might be of some use helping these kids get over their fears." She sighed and added under her breath, "Men!"

George had turned his back to her and was trying to resume his sleeping position.

"Never mind him, boys, everything will be all right. The conductor will find out what to do." She opened her purse and pulled out a package of Black Cat cigarettes. She opened it, removed a cigarette and dug in her purse again until she came up with a lighter. She took a long drag, held the smoke in and then slowly let it seep out through her lips and nostrils. It seemed to have a soothing effect on her, and I wished I could have one too. I liked smoking, but didn't get many opportunities to do so. Once in a while, I could snitch some of my mother's or Alexi's cigarettes.

I watched her totally enjoy her smoke, and she said, "My name is Myrna, by the way. We are going down to Toronto to visit my mother. George is already grumpy about that, but what I say is that I have rights too. I haven't seen my mother in over a year, and I have lived up in that no-man's land with only the company of his family. Why should he be the only one who sees his family?" She took another long drag. She seemed to have forgotten about our problems and instead focused on hers.

I just sat there and watched her cigarette, hypnotized. She finally put out her smoke and turned back around in her seat.

Fatigue and insecurity swallowed me like a tidal wave as I realized that I didn't know how to run my own life separate from the adults of the world. They had the reins. Now we were not only away from our home, but we had lost Paul. We even missed Arthur who, in some strange way, had become a kind of anchor in our mixed up lives.

The conductor finally headed back down the aisle toward us. He smiled as he approached and said, "Don't you worry, my boys, we will be in the next town in about thirty minutes. The engineer had radioed ahead, and the RCMP would be waiting for you to take you to your train. Your train has been radioed too and has stopped at a railway siding to wait for you."

Myrna turned around and smiled at us. "See, I told you everything would be all right."

Eventually, the train stopped, and the police came and took us to the right train, which was being held up for us. Arthur was frantic. We were relieved. We slept soundly, and I doubt that Arthur slept at all after that. He probably thought he would never sleep again. Poor Arthur.

9

The next day, we had a two and a half-hour wait in Pembrook. Arthur herded us from the train and into the local police station. He sat us down on chairs at the desk in front of the cop sitting on the other side and asked him to watch us until he came back. He hurried out of the door before the cop had a chance to respond. The policemen looked at us in bewilderment and asked, "What is this all about then?"

We shrugged our shoulders in unison, and Paul picked up the stapler from the desk. The cop took it from him and said to Paul, "What's your name young fellow?"

"Paul," said Paul.

The door opened, and Arthur was back. He had a small paper bag from which he extracted a long pair of skate laces. The policeman watched in amusement while he tied us together by the wrists.

I looked down at the tidy bow that he had tied between Peter and me, looked at Arthur, and smiled. Arthur caught the smile and said, "Don't *even* think about it."

He turned to the cop and said, "I can't keep these kids together, thanks for watching them." He then directed us out of the door and back to the train station.

We boarded the train and hung our heads like the convicted felons we were, tied together. Everyone on the train laughed, thinking that this was some kind of kids' game. Arthur's face was that lovely shade of red, and he seemed even older than he had at the onset of the trip.

Of course, we had to use the washroom and Arthur had to untie us to facilitate this. We made a scene when he tried to rejoin our wrists and Arthur, who seemed to shy away from public displays, had to give us our liberty.

Once in Ottawa, we had to leave the train. The remainder of the trip would be taken by bus. Arthur got scheduling information while we ran around like dogs that had escaped their leashes. Arthur managed to gather us together again, and we approached the revolving doors that were to give us our egress. Arthur eyed the door. After having been exposed to us for more than a couple of days, he seemed to think that the door represented some kind of threat. We decided to give Arthur a break and did not attempt to escape.

Arthur relaxed a bit as we got onto the bus. We ran to the back of the bus and, as people got on, separating us from Arthur, we jumped out of the side door. The bus took off, and we waved to Arthur, who stopped the bus and yelled at us to come back to him. We did, slowly, and Arthur did not seem to be very happy. Even his mustache dropped. Poor Arthur.

10

At nine in the evening, we arrived at the school. Over the door of the large building was a stature of St. Joseph, holding a small child.

Arthur said, "This will be your home of a while. You will be treated well and learn to be nice young gentlemen." Arthur uttered this statement with little conviction, and probably thought that anything short of a miracle would make this an impossible endeavor.

As we entered the main hallway, a dark-haired, middle-aged man came to greet us. The most extraordinary thing about him was that he was wearing a long black robe. His eyes pierced into us and his smile was a bit fierce, but his words seemed friendly enough.

"Welcome, boys, I am Brother Gordon, director of the school," he said with a smile. "This is the first time that we have had three brothers come to us at one time."

Behind him was a very small and gnomelike man who had to be at least sixty years old. He was smiling and waving at us. He too was wearing a long black robe.

"This is Brother Alvin," said the director. "He is the school nurse and runs the infirmary. If you are sick or hurt, he will be the one who will look after you."

As Brother Alvin's warm smile lit up his impish face, our fears of the unknown were set aside.

My brothers and I looked around the massive hall, and the strange men whose attention was focused on us. The director smiled benevolently at us, seeming to understand our nervousness. Paul clung to my side, and Peter was very close to me on the other side.

"Arthur and I will go to the office and sort out the paperwork," said the director. "Meanwhile, Brother Alvin will show you where you will sleep. Most of the boys are asleep already."

He turned to Arthur and asked, "Did everything go all right, Arthur? You look a little disheveled."

Arthur mumbled something, and they wandered down the hall together.

We followed Brother Alvin up a massive staircase and were led into a very large dormitory. There seemed to be hundreds of beds in the dorm. Brother Alvin explained that tonight's sleeping arrangements were temporary, and my brothers and I were given three beds together. Proper sleeping arrangements would be made in the morning. This was a relief to me since I was worried about my younger brothers on our first night, and didn't think it would be a good idea for us to be separated, especially Paul who was still quivering with fear and homesickness, and clinging to my arm like a wet shirt.

On each bed, there was a small pile of clothes consisting of a white shirt, one pair of gray trousers, a navy pullover sweater, and gym shorts. Brother Alvin told us to put these things in the locker under the bed. He then pulled the covers back for us, telling us to get undressed and into bed. He took our regular clothes and said that they would be kept in a locked cupboard until it was time for us to leave.

There had been no mention of the duration of our visit here, and I didn't have the nerve to ask, knowing that the information would upset me further, no matter how short or long the visit might be. I knew that if I was upset it would affect my brothers, and they would be more scared than they already were. There was no mention of us "Turning around and going home," as my mother had led us to believe might happen.

Once he saw us in bed and tucked in, Brother Alvin smiled with a broad grin, his eyes sparkling, and he patted us each on the head, and then he was gone. We whispered among ourselves for a few minutes, but we were all pretty exhausted. It took me no time to fall asleep, but it wasn't long before I woke up to the sound of Paul crying.

"What's wrong?" I asked.

"I want to go home. I want Mama," he sobbed and added, "I want Crystal and John."

"Shhh," I whispered. "Come over here and get in bed with me." I moved over and pulled the covers back for him to get in. Paul crawled in and fell asleep immediately.

The next thing I heard was the ringing of a loud bell. Soon, another long robe appeared hovering over my bed.

"Sleeping together is against the rules. There will be no sleeping together here. You have come here to get straightened out, and that is what is going to happen." He was tall and thin, he had an angular gaunt face with dark greasy hair. His eyes were cold and hard, and I could find no comfort in his presence. This, I learned later, was Brother René.

(So much for the warm, compassionate, understanding of the night before.)

"Now get up, it is time to get showered and dressed and then go to Mass," he snarled, showing yellow teeth.

In the center of the room, that was tiled from ceiling to floor, was a square partition. On each of the four sides of the partition, there were five showerheads. The floor sloped toward the partition slightly, and there were drains on each of the four sides. We lined up and waited our turn. Twenty boys were in the shower at one time. The younger boys showered first, so when I waited in line, I could observe the process. Four brothers walked around the perimeter of the shower room watching the boys, and some of them seemed to take more than a casual interest in the boys' bodies. They would touch the boys telling them to wash here or there, always here or there, being the most private parts of their bodies. When we got to the front of the line, another brother ordered us to strip and put our underwear into a large laundry bag that hung on a metal frame. The water was lukewarm. The soap was harsh, and the shampoo was in dispensers on the tiled walls. It stung the eyes and matted the hair.

Once showered, we lined up again for towels, and the brothers wiped the younger boys dry, taking longer than necessary over some. I watched closely when Paul, then Peter was in the shower and when they got out. They didn't seem to receive any unwarranted attention. A long walk-in cupboard contained metal shelves with clean sheets, towels, pillowcases, undergarments and shirts. We were directed to the linen cupboard to get clean underwear and then to our beds to get dressed. Our beds had to be made, and when we were finished, we had to stand next to them and wait for a brother to come and inspect the job.

Brother René came and pulled the covers off of Peter and Paul's beds.

"You two will be moving." He asked two of the older boys to move their beds. Paul's was moved to one end of a row. This row of beds was five rows over from mine. Peter's bed was moved three rows over from mine. One of the boys who moved Paul's bed instructed him how to make the bed properly, and Peter managed to get his done with a little help from a kid who was in the next bed in that row.

I was left standing next to Brother René, who pulled all of the bedding off of my bed.

"Haven't you ever made a bed on your own?" he sneered at me.

"Yes," I said. I didn't tell him that I sometimes pulled the covers up if Mama was coming up for an inspection. She always made the beds on washday, so that I never had to tuck the bedding in or start from scratch.

When everyone's bed met with Brother René's approval, we lined up again next to our beds. I had a chance to look around at the other boys and noticed that they seemed to go through the motions automatically. They all had very short hair, brush cuts. I realized, indignantly that they would probably shear us in the same manner. Some of the boys were dressed in the same clothing as I had been given, and others had put on coveralls over these clothes.

There was a kid two beds down staring at me. He looked familiar, but I couldn't place him. When René had moved across the room to chastise someone else, I heard the kid say, "Psst, is that you, Robin? Remember me from Welford?"

"Quiet down there!" shouted Brother René.

That was who he was. He had been in my class in grades three and four. His name was Eddy and his family had moved there when his father had transferred to work there with the provincial police. If you get put in here when your father was a cop, you must have really done something wrong.

Once everyone was assembled, we went to Mass. Eddie jumped back in the line to talk to me.

"This is great!" he said enthusiastically. "I'm glad there is someone here that I know."

I didn't know how he could say that it was great when we were both being held hostage at some idiot place with a bunch of guys running around in long, black robes.

There was a small chapel in the middle of the second floor. It turned out that there was another dorm on the other side of the chapel. We stood for Mass, which lasted about five minutes. I let my mind wander during Mass. I didn't know what was being said anyway since it was all in Latin.

After Mass, we lined up and went downstairs to the gym. Eddie whispered that he would see me later and ran ahead, not going to the gym. The boys wearing the coveralls lined up on one side of the gym, and one of the brothers called out their names and took them out of the building.

The director came into the gym and announced our arrival, introducing us as the "Three Le Blanc brothers." He then approached us and asked us to come down to the office before breakfast so that he could acquaint us with the rules and activities.

We followed him down the hall and wondered what horrors were in store for us until our mother came and fixed up this big misunderstanding. Once we reached his office, he told us to sit down, and he sat behind a large, heavy desk. Behind him was a large picture of the Pope and on the wall by the door was a plaster Jesus hanging on the cross. It made me depressed. It seemed to represent a threat of punishment.

"We will try to make your first day as simple as possible for you while you get your bearings and find your way around. The school runs a fair-sized farming operation as well as being a learning institution. There are cows, chickens, and pigs in the barns at the bottom of the hill. We also have a large maple syrup operation that everyone works at in the spring. We grow vegetables in the fields for our own consumption, and everyone is assigned a job. Your jobs for now will probably not be the same a week from now, but until we decide where to place you, Robin, you will work with the chickens cleaning the coops. Peter, you will be working with the pigs, feeding and helping with the slopping of the sties."

Peter, who had smirked when he heard my job of cleaning chicken coops, now looked disgusted and about to protest. I lowered my head so that he couldn't see my smile.

The director now looked at Paul. "You, young man, will be in charge of cleaning the blackboards in the three classrooms on the east side of the building. You will also clean the brushes for these classrooms.

Peter was now looking really miffed. I couldn't help but snicker.

"Do you have a problem, Robin," the director asked me.

"No, sir," I said hanging my head.

"Good," he looked down at the papers on his desk. "After morning chores, everyone goes to breakfast in the large dining room. You will be shown your seats by one of the brothers looking after the dining room. That will be either Brother René or Brother Jacob. After breakfast, there is time to change from your working clothes before going to class. Robin and

Peter, you will be given coveralls for chores. You Robin will be placed in grade five, Peter in grade three, and Paul in grade two."

"We also have a lot of sports at the school, and we take them seriously. I don't know if you play hockey, baseball, or football; but we have several teams of each, and we compete with different schools in the area. Of course, we are now in hockey season and our A Team is number one in the district. If you are interested in any sports, you can arrange with the teacher to try out for the team. Right now, you will all be taken to see Brother Alvin, who is the barber as well as nurse and counselor.

We followed the director up the stairs to the second floor infirmary. Here, we found Brother Alvin, with his gnomelike grin, surrounded with more religious icons on the wall than I have ever seen in one spot. He gave us a beaming smile, and I had a sinking feeling as I spotted the clippers. Peter groaned out loud and Paul didn't seem to care.

"Who is going to be my first customer?" asked Brother Alvin.

"I'll leave you to it then, Brother Alvin," said the director. "Could you show them to the dining room when you have finished with their hair?"

"I can do that," said the seemingly ever-cheerful man. "Now then, who is going to be first?"

Paul walked over and got into the waiting chair. Brother Alvin put a cape around Paul's neck and beamed at him, "You are a brave little fellow, now aren't you?"

Paul just smiled and settled down. I looked around the room. In one corner, there was a cot, with a rocking chair next to it. There was a small table and a large glass-fronted cupboard standing against one wall. It seemed to be full of bottles and bandages. There was also an examining table like the ones in the doctors' offices. There were a couple of wooden chairs other than the one Paul was sitting on. Some books had been put under him so that Brother Alvin didn't have to stoop to cut his hair. The clippers were running through Paul's hair, amputating his blond curls, making him unrecognizable. Paul looked over at Peter and me and smiled at our shocked faces.

"Now maybe you won't think of me as a baby. Mama always made me have long curls and now I don't have to be cute." He already had found some positive elements in the school, and I was shocked at the transformation of his appearance.

As Brother Alvin shook out the cape and looked questioningly at us, I stepped bravely over to the chair. If my baby brother could do it, so could I. I still marveled at Paul, who we had all called "Baby" for so long. Mama still did. He never let on that he had disliked it; he always had been so cheerful and happy. He had never said how he felt.

I felt the vibration of the clippers as they mowed my head, hair dropping on the floor in great heaps I bit my lip trying to think of anything else, to avoid crying. God, this would be humiliating if I cried, and Paul had been so brave. What the heck, hair grows. It wasn't as if everyone else here didn't have the same thing, but I was still thinking that I would be out of here in not time, and the kids at school would give me a hard time over my haircut.

Once we were all shorn, Brother Alvin took us down to the dining hall. He learned from Brother René where our seats were. We were put in different areas, the dining room being divided up into tables according to the age and grade of the person. We had to stand behind our appointed chairs until grace was said. We then lined up to get our breakfast consisting of porridge and toast. Milk glasses were on the table, and there were large pitchers of milk placed on the table.

When I got to the front of the line, I held out my bowl and looked up to see Eddy there serving porridge.

"Hi," he said with a smile. He put a spoonful of porridge in my bowl and saw me wince. "Don't you like oatmeal?"

"Not really," I said.

He dipped the spoon back in my bowl and took most of it out. "You have to have some, and you have to clean the bowl, so I'll only give you a little, put lots of sugar on it, and you will find it tastes better. There is lots of toast, and you can have as much as you want."

I went back to my seat and ate in silence.

There was lots of fresh butter as well. Later I found out that this, along with the milk were produced right there at the school. It reminded me of Crystal and John. Meals were to be taken without speaking, and this rule was strictly enforced. I wondered how Eddy got a job in the kitchen and found the idea of a guy doing the cooking kind of funny. I guessed that this was probably because there weren't any women or girls there to do the job.

When breakfast was finished, Brother Rene said something in Latin, and the boys were required to say "Gratis" in unison. This strict and structured repast was a far cry from the chaos we were accustomed to at breakfast time at home.

We went to the gym hall next and stayed there until nine o'clock when classes began. The class I was placed in held the French-speaking grades five to eight. I was anxious about being separated from my two brothers. Their teacher, Brother Beacon, had come to the gym to meet them and take them to their classroom. He seemed to pick up on my fears and tried to reassure me that he would take good care of them. Around fifty-five years old, short and fat, Brother Beacon presented a friendly countenance. His head was fringed with gray hair, and there was a large bald spot on the top of his head. He had a round smooth face and big brown eyes. His cheeks were rosy, and he reminded me of a beardless Santa. He came over to me with a smile that, if it wasn't for his ears, would have gone all the way around his head.

"Don't worry about your brothers, I will look after them." His smile made his eyes dance, and I relaxed a bit and hoped that he was as kind as he seemed.

Later, my brothers reported to me that Brother Beacon was a funny, kind man, and that they both liked him a lot.

My teacher was Brother Stephen. He was probably in his midthirties, tall and fairly muscular. He had medium brown hair and brown eyes flecked with gold. Although his face was not exactly handsome, it was strong and assuring. He gave me some academic testing and decided that I should be placed in grade six instead of grade five, saying that I would probably not find much challenge in the grade five classes. This was fine with me.

Later, I had learned that Peter had been tested and put into grade four.

Eddy was in the sixth grade, and I was seated in front of him. I found some comfort in having someone familiar there. I didn't remember much about him from before, but I thought that he and I would probably be close friends, even if he worked cooking—and if my mother didn't rescue me in a hurry.

Brother Stephen seemed to be liked and respected by the other boys in my class. He was able to make jokes and get a laugh from the boys, and he made it look easy to have the control of the class. I made these assessments unconsciously and immediately trusted him I had no trouble fitting into the classroom routine and found that I quite enjoyed it. It helped that Eddy was there.

11

We returned to the dining hall for lunch at noon, and Brother Rene introduced us to Brother Jacob, who assisted Brother Rene as one of our prefects. Brother Jacob would also be teaching gym and sports. He alternated meal supervision with Brother Rene.

Brother Jacob was the youngest brother, being in his early twenties. His wavy blond hair formed a helmet around his face, which was long and angular. He had a straight narrow nose and eyes the color of amethyst. He was beautiful instead of handsome, and his clean face seemed less a result of shaving than a lack of need. He smiled and said, "I am going to enjoy working with you. I am sure we will get along fine." He put his arm around my shoulder, and I felt very uncomfortable. I squirmed out of his grasp and muttered something in response. The lunch routine was the same as that at breakfast.

Following lunch, we returned again to the gym, where we were put through rigorous exercises for half an hour. Brother Jacob and Brother Rene stood in the center of the gym watching as we performed sit-ups, push-ups, and jumped ropes. We then ran five laps around the gym as Brother Rene shouted at the boys moving too slow for his liking. He stepped up to the circle and grabbed one boy by the collar and threw him to the floor.

"You lazy tub of lard, move your butt or lose it!" Rene kicked him in the butt, and the boy curled into a ball. Everyone in the gym tried to avert their eyes while continuing the last lap around the room. Brother Jacob smiled as he watched the boy on the floor. Brother Rene kicked him a few more times and then stepped back. He looked at Brother Jacob, and they smiled at each other.

To my surprise, the boy got to his feet and said meekly, "Thank you, Brother Rene."

When we finished our running, I asked the boy standing next to my why the kid had said thank you.

"When you are punished, you have to say thank you," he said. "You are punished because you have done something wrong, and you are supposed to be glad that they have corrected you so that you will turn into a better person."

I thought that he was joking and looked at his face. There was nothing to indicate that he thought this was funny; in fact, I think he may even have believed in this philosophy.

Brother Jacob then said, "Everyone, sit down on the floor, and we will have our half hour of meditation." He glanced and me and must have seen my confusion since I hadn't heard this word before. "For the new boys, this means that we have thirty minutes to think." He smiled at me and winked.

I wondered how a person decides to think. Or rather how did a person stop from thinking? It seemed to me that I thought all the time, and I wondered if this was unusual. Did they mean something other than the activity that I had given this name? I had been thinking since my arrival.

Finally, we were allowed fifteen minutes of talking time. It was okay not to talk if you didn't feel like it, but I tried not to look like I was thinking.

We went back to the afternoon classes after this. Classes were a pleasant change, and I found that Brother Stephen challenged his students, making us use our imaginations and asking questions.

We returned to the gym for the time between classes and supper. This was a slightly less structured time, but if you wanted to join any teams (baseball, hockey, etc), you would have this time for practice or games. Some of the boys had chores, and they put their overalls back on.

That first evening, a couple of boys were having an argument about the score in their pool game. Brother Rene ran across the room, grabbed one of the boys by the throat, and threw him on the pool table. He then punched him in the face, and when the boy struggled to get up, he was thrown on the floor and kicked in the face and ribs. I looked on in horror, and my younger brothers came and hid behind me. We had never seen this kind of cruelty even when we saw some of the town drunks fighting.

Paul started to cry. "I don't want him to do that to us," he whimpered.

Brother Rene was not finished with his sadistic form of discipline yet. He next grabbed the second boy involved, who had been cowering over by the window, and pushed him. The boy stumbled and banged his head on the window ledge and slid to the floor. He pulled his knees up to his chin and covered his face with his hands. Brother Rene gave him a swift kick in the shins and turned away. Blood was streaming from behind the boy's ear, and he was crying.

Brother Rene turned back and said, "I didn't hear you, boy!"

"Thank you, Brother Rene," mumbled the boy. He wiped his face with the back of his sleeve and got up slowly on shaky legs.

I couldn't look at the boy. I felt his shame and embarrassment and didn't want to add to it by staring.

By now, Paul was crying with great sobs and burying his face under my arm. I watched Brother Rene's rage surreptitiously. His face was a blood red, his nostrils flared, his eyes were wide open and unblinking, the whites showing around the irises and pupils dilated.

"Don't worry, Paul," I said with an assurance that I didn't feel, and hiding my shock as best I could. "I will die before I let them do anything like that to you. I promise."

Sometime in our second week, we were having lunch in the dining hall, and I got my own introduction to Brother Rene's disfavor.

"Could you pass the salt," I asked the boy next to me.

Brother Rene appeared behind me and pulled me off my chair.

"There is no talking during meals," he shouted.

"I was only asking for the salt," I protested.

He threw me on the floor and started kicking me in the ribs. He then grabbed me by the hair and flung me back into the chair.

"Maybe now you will learn to listen and obey," he shouted, his eyes flaring, and he was panting with the exertion. The shock and embarrassment I felt at that moment quickly turned to humiliated anger and hatred.

I was learning. The seed of hatred had been germinated, and it burned in my gut and took root. Frustrated rage at my helplessness engulfed me, and I blinked back the tears that burned my eyes. My face was red hot and my childish mind cried for revenge. I longed for the day that I would no longer be helpless and would be the one with the reins to control my own life.

12

The school was split in two sections. The senior boys were in one section, and the junior boys in the other. Boys up to the age of fifteen were in the junior section and boys older than fifteen were in the senior section. Entering the main door at the front of the building, on your right was the junior side and to the left was the senior boys' side. One side was the mirror of the other. Each end of the main floor held a gym, games room, and dining room for the brothers, kitchen, locker room and dining hall for the boys. There were stairs leading up to the dorms on the second floor. The second floor had on each side a sleeping dorm; shower room; visiting salon; infirmary; a small glass-sided room off the dorm for observation, and the director's office was located in the center front, dividing the two areas.

In the dorm, the beds were lined up in rows. The row in which you slept was determined by your age. At the back of the second floor was a walkway that led across to the building behind. This building housed the brothers' rooms, each containing a bed, dresser, desk and chair, each room being an office as well as sleeping quarters. On the third floor were the classrooms and library, and a large hall for assemblies.

There were classrooms for English-speaking kids, and classrooms for the French-speaking kids. Most of our classes and assemblies were for one language or the other. Our sports were sometimes intermingled, and sometimes adversarial.

The assembly room and the chapel were not duplicated, so at some of the assemblies, we got to see the older boys. At all other times, the two sides behaved like two separate schools.

There were two massive, roaring furnaces in the basement with their tentacles reaching out to all corners of the building like bloated octopuses. These had to be fed with coal that was delivered down the back lane. It came down the chute and into the coal scuttle. The doors of these monsters were huge and heavy. When opened, the blast of heat that emanated from the inferno within would make your eyelashes stick together, and your face burn feverishly. The glare of light that shone out of the open doors made you feel like you were dealing with an angry god who would escape and wreak havoc on the building.

The maintenance man oversaw the furnaces, and he usually had two senior boys helping shovel the coal. This job was not regularly assigned to the same two boys. There was a roster that designated a different team of boys every week.

The basement also held old dishes, old holy pictures, furniture, and books, storage lockers, extra canned food supplies, and lots of mice and some rats. These vermin seemed immune to the rat bane set out for them, and they flourished.

In the playing field, there were two baseball diamonds and two football fields, and at either end of the building there was a skating rink in the winter—one for the juniors and one for the seniors.

There was another field at the bottom of the hill. A barn housing cows, pigs and a coop for chickens filled the center of the field. The school had a lucrative farming set up and was close to self-sufficient. The boys were expected to help with the care of the livestock, milking the cows and collecting the eggs.

Between the main building and the field down the hill was a pond.

The sugar bush, which was located behind the playing field, was our spring activity. The maple syrup season had just finished when we arrived. The production of maple syrup was the most profitable of all the enterprises. It was a large set up that was run with the efficiency of a factory. The sap ran from the spigots in the trees directly into tubes that linked to each of the trees. The tube ran directly into large drums. Horse and cart transported these drums to the bottom of the hill where a constant fire was burning. Great cauldrons hung over the fire, and the sap bubbled away until it was reduced to syrup.

Life offered a variety of activities and chores at the school. There was little time for idling, apart from sports and doing schoolwork, we had to work in the farming operation.

13

My twelfth birthday came and went without any of the usual hoopla in that first month of residency. My mother sent a card, but it was a day late. I was determined not to show my feelings to anyone. Even my brothers didn't know it was my birthday. They probably never did know the date. In the past, my mother probably just told them on that day. The only acknowledgment came in the form of the director's daily birthday announcements over the PA. This was followed by unenthusiastic applause from the others and that was the end of it.

I cried myself to sleep that night. I was overwhelmed with self-pity and anger. It was May, and I had joined the baseball team. Sports were a diversion, and I could work out my anger, aggression, and energy as I immersed myself in competition.

While out playing baseball one day, I ran from first to second base where I bumped into the kid playing the base. Brother Rene ran out to me and screamed, "You did that on purpose, you brat!"

"I didn't," I contradicted.

Rene grabbed me and punched me, knocking me to the ground. He kept kicking me harder and harder until I mercifully passed out.

Gradually, my consciousness returned. I was afraid to open my eyes. I lay still, listening, realizing that I was in some kind of a bed. I opened my eyes slowly and painfully. Brother Alvin was fretting over me. When he saw that I was awake he said, "You poor, poor, boy. Who did this to you?" He gently brushed the hair off my bruised face.

"Brother Rene," I said dully. Already, I realized that Brother Rene was a law unto himself, and he seemed to be able to carry out any horrendous act with complete impunity.

Brother Alvin mumbled to himself, "Brother Rene . . . Mad Dog." His usual smiling face took on a look of frustrated rage. I felt a kinship with him then. He was too old and feeble to fight the likes of Brother Rene, and I was too young, small, and weak to fight him. We were always conscious of his presence, even when we couldn't see him. He would seemingly fly out of nowhere and attack for any misdemeanor, real or otherwise. I began to think he had evil powers, with the ability to travel through space and time. It was like being in a deep hole of darkness that, when there was a glimmer of light at the top, and you managed to claw your way up to the lip, you were pushed back down.

I stayed in the infirmary that night. Around ten in the evening, Brother Jacob showed up to see how I was doing. "How are you feeling now, Robin?" he asked with great solicitude.

"I am better now," I said.

He put his hand on my thigh and said, "You and I will become friends, and I won't let this happen to you any more."

"Thanks," I whispered, feeling a little better.

At that moment, with Brother Alvin's and Brother Jacob's seeming concern and understanding of Rene's evilness, I thought maybe the side of good would eventually prevail and that one evil person would surely be outnumbered.

"You get some sleep now, and we will talk about this later," said Brother Jacob, taking his leave.

I slept peacefully, and in the morning, Brother Alvin gave me some words of advice. "Be very, very, careful Robin. Don't talk back, even when you are being unfairly treated or accused. Do not look directly into Brother Rene's eyes, he will take it as a challenge. He is stronger than you are, and you will not come out the winner of any battle with him. He is very cruel and sadistic."

"No shit!" I thought.

"Get dressed, and we will go for a walk."

We walked down to the sugar bush. Brother Alvin's eyes were filled with sadness as he told me how he had come here to help young boys get their lives on the right track. He looked old and disappointed. He seemed to feel personally responsible for the evil of others. His grief was a kind of mourning, and I saw him differently.

The light that filtered through the leaves seemed to congregate around his small frame, giving him a body-length aura, making him seem larger and unworldly. At that moment, I thought that he and he alone had been sent directly from God and not from the human race.

"It doesn't seem that the things they do to us here are going to help us be better people," I commented. "It seems that what is done to us here only makes us mean and unhappy."

"I do not like to see children beaten and abused, and there is nothing I can do to prevent it. All I can do is be there when it happens and try to patch them up and comfort them. I can only work on the external injuries. The inner scars, I have no way of fixing other than showing that there is another, kinder side to mankind. I can only hope that most of you boys will make the decision to care instead of hate, although I cannot blame a boy for developing hatred when he has been exposed to the abuse that goes on here. For some reason, God has included evil in this world," Brother Alvin said this as if he alone bore the weight of the world's sins.

"I will tell you this one real truth," he continued. "If you hate someone, that person owns you. They will eat at your soul and destroy the goodness and joy that you possess. They will take time from you while you are thinking of them, hating them."

Brother Alvin looked around and said, "It is like a beautiful painting here. It is like an exquisite wall hanging, but if you move it, you see that it covers a large, ugly, scarred surface. It is only an impression of beauty, not the real thing. I try to see the perfection in His plan, but the element of evil, I can only explain to myself as a kind of test of our strength and goodness.

"I come here to the sugar bush," he continued, "when things get hard for me to understand. It breaks my heart to see some of the things that I see going on here, and I try to tell myself that it is part of larger plan. I must confess, I am not wise enough to always see the Plan." He sighed.

"People like Brother Rene do not belong here. He does not represent what this place is meant to be. You boys are lost little angels who have strayed and need to be guided back gently, not beaten senseless, creating fear and hatred in the wake of abuse."

Sadness seemed to engulf him. How Brother Alvin had managed to keep his idealism even though he was living in the midst of rampant brutality was a mystery to me.

We walked and talked for about two hours. The more he talked, the more I became aware he was trying to comfort himself as well as me.

I could have spent the rest of the day with him in that sugar bush. Although he realized I was a child, he talked to me as he would an equal—as if he had respect for me as a person. I could not identify this phenomenon at the time, since it was the first time in my life that this had happened to me. But I did not have the option of spending the rest of the day there. It was time to return to the fold and the shepherds. My time of sanctuary was over, and I tried to draw from Brother Alvin the strength I needed to face my world again.

14

One day in June, I was told to go to Brother Jacob's room off the dorm. I went up to his room, and he greeted me with a smile.

"Come in, Robin," he said, shutting the door behind me and locking it, explaining, "This way, we will not be disturbed while we talk."

My stomach churned, and I could feel my scalp begin to itch as sweat began to flow. I said nothing and waited.

"Do you remember when I talked to you in the infirmary, Robin," he asked.

"Yes," I said quietly.

"Well," he took me by the shoulders and stood in front of me, and then he embraced me. "We have to be nice to each other and love one another, and I will protect you." He pulled me closer, and I felt the pressure of his erection against my belly.

"No!" I shouted, pushing him away trying to suppress the nausea rising in me.

His face became red with anger, and he removed his robe. "Look at me, Robin. See how beautiful I am? Don't you want to touch me? I am sure you will enjoy the pleasures we can give each other."

"No! Let me out of here! I want to go downstairs!" I cried out.

The revulsion on my face was evident, and Jacob's smile turned into an ugly scowl of rage over my rejection. He slapped my face and hissed through his teeth, "You are making a big mistake, Robin. You do not want me for an enemy. I will see that you regret this. Now get out!"

I was through the door before he could change his mind. I belted down the stairs without a backward glance, feeling lucky to have escaped and not knowing what form the repercussions would take, but knowing that I would have to pay dearly.

15

On the first Monday of every month, we would go to the third floor hall. At this time the previous month's records would be read. The boys were slotted into three categories—excellent, good, or bad. If you fell into the latter category, you were sent to the director's office.

The crimes that would earn you the label of *bad* could be anything from talking during quiet times, having bad grades, having your bed made improperly, or any number of things that struck the brothers' idea of insubordination or misbehavior.

Once in the director's office, you would be ordered to bare your ass and lean over the desk. You would be given five to eight lashes of the strap, depending on the magnitude of your badness. The strap had rough grooves that would not only leave welts, but cut your skin as well. On those Mondays some of the boys could be heard screaming through the halls, others would faint.

On one of those Mondays, there were no *bad boys* to report. The director stared unbelievingly, and then he screamed, "You brothers are not doing your jobs! It is impossible that there are no bad boys this month." He raged for quite a while.

The next month, this oversight was rectified and there were twelve bad boys. The director was all smiles. I began to realize the nature of his perversion even though I didn't understand it at the time.

Beatings turned out to be a regular sport, especially for Brother Rene. He would leave in his wake broken noses, ribs, blackened eyes, split lips, broken glasses, bruised and ruptured kidneys and numerous broken bones.

One boy was so badly injured, he needed eye surgery. The doctor was told that the injury was the result of a hockey injury.

One way to avoid the abuse was to become a brother's lover. There were eight or ten boys who took this option, and although it gave them immunity to the beatings, it alienated them from their peers. These boys would go off with one of the brothers and return with candy, chips, or some other treat and flaunt them to the rest of us. The brothers would be around these boys all the time. (Like flies around a pile of shit.)

The smaller boys would be taken off by the brothers and would return crying, often with blood on the seats of their pants. You could see the fear and pain on their faces, or sometimes they just stared vacantly into space. We were helpless and unable to do anything to change the situation.

This was part of the daily regimen, and we were at the mercy of our guardians. Everyone lived in perpetual fear. The horror and threat of rape or beatings was constant. One never relaxed. The brothers taunted us with threats, knowing how debilitating our fear was. This ensured their power over us and kept us in this unvarying state of unease.

Anticipating the infliction of pain, as one would wait for a needle, is indeed terrifying, far more terrifying than unexpected or accidental pain or injury.

The brothers knew this and our fear was another source of pleasure for them. It was like holding a gun to our head each day and pulling the trigger. Sometimes, the chamber was loaded, and others, it was not. This depended on which sadistic pleasure needed sating on that particular day; inflicting pain, sexual gratification, or seeing us grovel and cower in fear. The feast table for the barbaric brothers was laden with so many boys that there was a never-ending supply of bodies. If one of the dishes needed replenishing, it was sent to the infirmary and repatched, then returned to the table for further consumption.

16

The day after the incident with Brother Jacob, I was still shaken. I found it hard to concentrate on my work, and my brothers found me too distracted to communicate.

That day, we had another baseball game. My position was third base, and I was usually a better than average player. That day, however, I could do nothing right. I fumbled balls, and every time I was up to bat, I struck out. At the end of the game, as I was putting away some gear, Brother Jacob came over to me and shouted loud enough for everyone to hear.

"You blew the game on purpose! You will be punished for that. You will receive five lashes with the strap." With that, he turned to the other boys and said, "If any of you have the idea of throwing a game, you will get the same treatment."

He turned back to me and said, "Up to my room right now."

I went up to his room with great trepidation. My fear was less for the strap, but what else he might have in store for me. Time passed slowly as I waited for the inevitable. Jacob took his time in order to heighten my terror and weaken my defenses. I was trembling with fear when he entered.

When he was finally in the room he looked at me and smiled. "It doesn't have to be like this, Robin. You know that you do not have to have the strap if you decide to love me instead. I do not really want to hurt you; I only want to be allowed to love you."

"No!" I screamed, knowing that no one would come to my rescue.

"Very well then," he said, "Drop your pants and lay on the bed."

I did as I was told slowly and lay face down on his bed. Nothing happened for a minute, and I turned to see him disrobing. His arousal was evident as he grabbed up the strap. He lifted it above his head and brought it down hard on my buttocks. His lips pulled back from his teeth giving him a predatory grin. He struck me again and again, and the strap came down harder and faster each time. He lost control, and the strap landed on my neck, on my back and on my thighs and calves. My skin was screaming in pain, and my tears were choking me. I couldn't get my breath, and my nose ran and eyes streamed. I don't know if I screamed or not.

After an eternity, Brother Jacob's rage was spent, and he ran out of steam, so the beating stopped.

"Each time you reject me, the beatings will be worse, and eventually you will let me have you," he said.

I said nothing. There was nothing that I could say that would improve the situation. I didn't have the strength to suffer the onslaught that would result if I said the words that were running through my head at the time.

I was finally allowed to get dressed. Along with blood on my legs, I noticed a sticky, milky fluid on the side of my legs. Brother Jacob was panting with exertion as he put his robe back on over his sweat-covered body. I moved with great difficulty down the stairs, and was unable to sit down. When we went to bed, my brothers saw my back and Paul cried with fear and a pain of his own. "Don't let them do that to you any more!" he cried.

"Don't worry, Paul, I won't," I said, biting back the tears and trying to smile and reassure him. "I'm tough."

But I didn't feel tough. In fact, I felt only fear. Fear was becoming a constant companion. The fear of punishment, beatings, and the threat of rape were probably worse than the actuality. Fear walked at my side every day. I didn't just have to fear for myself, I had to fear for my brothers. I also began to fear for my sanity. It seemed that my sanity was hanging by a thread, like a baby tooth that was ready to fall, hanging loosely by a minute piece of skin.

I told Brother Rene in the morning that I was unwell and that I was going to the infirmary. He looked at me, and I guess I looked sick enough for him to believe me, so he let me go.

Once inside the sanctuary of the infirmary and seeing Brother Alvin, I could finally release all my pent-up emotions and tears. My body shook with great racking sobs as I let down all pretense of bravery. Here, I didn't have to wear the mask that I felt was necessary in front of my brothers and peers. Here, I was safe. The relief of shedding the inhibiting restraint of bravado was as intense as breathing after holding your breath under water as long as you could.

Brother Alvin took one look at me and told me to take off my shirt. Seeing the welts o my back and neck, the tears welled up in his eyes as he put his arms around me. "You poor little angel," he said. "Why must these animals do this?" He didn't expect me to have an answer. He put salve on my wounds and tried with words to salve my emotions.

As he rocked and comforted me, I told him what had happened with Brother Jacob and why the beating was so severe. Brother Alvin was shocked and fearful.

"Robin, do not say a word of this to anyone. If you do, you will probably suffer even worse punishment than you've already seen. Let me see what I can do about the situation."

That afternoon, Brother Alvin came to the door of my classroom. He talked with Brother Stephen, and after class Brother Stephen asked me to stay behind. I sat at my desk and waited until there were just the two of us in the room.

"Robin, Brother Alvin has arranged for you to start working in the kitchen. Instead of going to the gym tomorrow morning, you will report to the kitchen. You will also leave classes an hour early at lunch. You will not be involved in the supper preparation since you are involved in sports, and there is another group of boys who make supper."

So now I knew how a guy got involved in cooking.

17

My first morning in the kitchen began at 5:00 a.m. Eddy greeted me at the door. By now, Eddy and I were fairly good friends. We played hockey and baseball together, and shared a lot of common interests.

There were six other boys in the kitchen all doing various chores. One was washing pots and loading the dishwasher. Two were chopping vegetables. One guy was putting butter and bread on plates. The last boy was filling glasses with milk and loading them onto a cart.

"Hey! Robin! I didn't know that you would be helping out in the kitchen. This is great! Come on, I'll show you what to do."

He took me to the cupboard and showed me where the aprons were.

"We have to wear these," he said, apologetically.

I groaned.

He laughed. "I know, but you get used to them after a while."

"I guess you can get used to anything," I said sadly.

He sensed that there was more behind my words than what I was saying.

"You meant the brothers?" he asked.

I didn't respond. My feelings were still too close to the surface to trust my voice.

"No," said Eddy, "You never get used to the brothers. They are straight from hell. You just try to keep out of their way. Did Brother Jacob beat you really bad with the belt after the game yesterday? I felt so helpless and wanted to attack him, but that wouldn't have done any good. I'm sorry."

I looked at him and realized that I wasn't alone and that I didn't have the corner on the market for mistreatment. A kinship was beginning to develop between us.

Our job was to put the vegetables into a pot with water and seasoning, and turn it into soup. There was supposed to be a brother overseeing the kitchen, but Eddy told me that he never came in unless there was a problem. His name was Brother Clarence, and he was old and spent a lot of time in his rooms.

"I would like to kill them," I whispered with guiltless conviction.

"Good luck," said Eddy. "You and everyone else. You can only dream about that. You wouldn't stand a chance."

I didn't say anything. I nursed thoughts of revenge and was positive one day I would be in a position to retaliate.

I learned that Eddy too had suffered at the hands of Rene and Jacob. We compared notes. His experiences had been similar to mine. We found that we had a common ground in our mutual festering hatred for most of the brothers. We agreed that Brothers Stephen, Alvin and Beacon were the only ones who were worth their salt. The rest were sent directly from Lucifer.

I was carrying a pot of soup to the dining room one lunch hour, where I was to serve it to the boys as they lined up with their bowls. I pushed through the swinging doors from the kitchen and saw Brother Rene beating one of the smaller boys. His eyes were glazed, pupils dilated and nostrils flaring—an expression I had grown to recognize. I was sorely tempted to pour the pot of scalding soup on him, but I resisted the urge.

"Excuse me please, *sir*," I said in my most respectful voice.

He looked at me and stopped his beating. The boy's face was bloody, and he was crying in pain. At first, I thought Brother Rene was going to come after me, but he must have seen the pot and realized that I was armed in some manner, so he moved aside. He glared at me, and I glared back. His breathing was labored, and he reminded me of a crazed bull.

After serving the boys their soup, I was to serve Rene his. I carried the steaming soup over to his table, my hands trembling as I approached him. I stared right at him, not removing my gaze for a second. He watched me and seemed to read my mind and knew what I wanted to do with the soup.

"Don't you even *think* about it!" he said.

I stood there while he glared at me, and I glared defiantly back for close to a minute. He lowered his eyes first. I was giddy when I returned to the kitchen and told Eddy what had happened.

"Are you nuts?" Eddy shouted. "He's a mad dog. He will kill you. Why don't you just shoot yourself? Don't do that, it isn't worth it." He ranted on for a few minutes like this.

"Okay, okay," I said but it had felt good to have been outwardly defiant and even have that speck of control over even one small situation. I realized that if I was armed I would have a fighting chance, but not one that would allow me to go unpunished. This incident sparked a glimmering of a plan to get some revenge on the brothers.

The next day, we were told to make two soups—pea soup for the boys and vegetable soup for the brothers.

"Eddy," I said, "The soup for the brothers has to be very spicy today."

"Why?" he asked.

"Just because, they will like it better." I smiled evilly at him.

"Who cares if they like it?" he asked.

"Trust me," I said.

When the soup was made, before adding the spices, I removed three bowls and set them aside. I put the soup pot on the floor, unzipped my pants and pissed in the soup. Eddy was scandalized.

"I can't believe you did that!" he cried. "I don't believe it!" He looked at the smirk on my face and eventually saw the humor in the situation. I stepped back from the pot and gestured for him to step right up and enjoy.

Eddy looked furtively around and then took my place at the pot and relieved himself. We quickly put the pot back on the stove giggling nervously.

"I wonder what it tastes like," mused Eddy.

"It's probably a bit salty," I said.

We reheated the three bowls of unadulterated soup before taking them out into the Brothers' dining room. We placed the three bowls on the trolley next to the pot and empty bowls. When we came to Brother Beacon, we served him one of the prepoured bowls and told him that we had taken some soup out before we added a lot of spice because we knew that he didn't like things too spicy. We did the same for Brother Stephen and Brother Alvin. Brother Alvin was suspicious and looked at my face, then at the soup pot, and then the bowl being presented to him. He smiled and shook his head as if to say, "No, no, no."

I smiled back at him and nodded, "Yes, yes, yes."

He took the bowl, still looking at the soup pot. He looked back and forth between his bowl, the soup pot, and me. Eddy and I kept our eyes down, not daring to look at one another. If the brothers caught the look that we would have passed between us, the gig would have been up.

"After you are done with your lunch chores, I want you to come up to the infirmary and have your medical," Brother Alvin said firmly.

"All right," I said, and went back to the kitchen barely containing my giggles. Eddy and I laughed and laughed, glimpsing through the door every once in a while to see if any of the brothers had dropped dead—no such luck.

I went up to see Brother Alvin and as soon as I was in the door he grabbed me by the arm and made me face him.

"What did you do to the soup?" he demanded.

"Nothing," I said innocently. "It had a lot of spice, like I said. I didn't think you would like it as spicy as that, so we took some out before the spice was added."

"Don't fool with me! What did you do?" His voice was getting shriller. Brother Alvin may have liked me, but he was nobody's fool and wasn't going to be duped by a twelve-year-old boy.

"I pissed in the soup," I relented.

"What?" Alvin sputtered and rented, "What? What?" He kept asking over and over, but not really expecting an answer since he had heard me perfectly well. "Don't you ever do anything like that again. May God forgive you. You better get out before I change my mind and give you a good hiding. You are a very bad boy."

As I turned to leave, I caught a glimpse of the smile that was creeping up into his eyes, and the sides of his mouth twitched. As the door closed behind me, I heard him laugh out loud for the first time. I could still hear him laughing as I descended the stairs.

Eddy was full of questions when I returned to the kitchen, and I told him what had transpired. Now it was his turn to sputter and rant. "We're dead," he said. "Why? Why? Why did I let you talk me into such a crazy thing?" He went on pacing and holding his head anxiously.

"But, Eddy," I cut in, "they loved the soup. Some had seconds. One of them even said, 'Mmmmmm, what good soup!'"

He looked at me in confusion, and then when what I had said penetrated, he grinned and finally broke out in a full-bellied laugh. We laughed all afternoon, tears running down our faces, gasping for breath. That evening, we only had to look at one another and start laughing all over.

It felt good to laugh. As we laughed, I realized that I hadn't really laughed since I had come to this godforsaken place four months ago. Our kinship and mutual hatred gave us courage. We were a small army of two, but for me, that one other person made the difference between being able to face my life each day and not. Daily, we became a little stronger, a little braver, and less at the mercy of our antagonists—if only in our minds. I hate to think what that place would have been like if I didn't have his friendship.

18

Winter came, and Eddy and I were on the all-star hockey team. We liked playing together, joking and laughing, enjoying the game and our now strong bond. During the game, Eddy lost the puck to the other side, and they scored the winning goal. After the game, Brothers Jacob and Rene were so angry that they picked Eddy up by each arm, dragged him into the gym, and attacked. They punched and kicked him, and then Brother Rene picked up a hockey stick and broke it across his back. Brother Rene was in a blind rage as he continued to beat Eddy with the broken stick, hitting every inch of Eddy's body even after he was unconscious. I could see boys peering around the door of the gym in fear.

I grabbed Jacob by the arm and shouted, "Stop him! Stop him!"

He looked down at me and got a sly grin on his face. "All right," he said, and he grabbed Brother Rene's wrist as he was about to strike Eddy again with the stick.

"You had better stop, Rene," he said quietly.

Brother Rene glanced at Brother Jacob in confusion as if he didn't know where he was, and he looked at the stick in his hand, still being restrained at the wrist by Brother Jacob. He peered down at the unconscious and bleeding form of Eddy, lying on the floor; then he saw me. Once spotting me, his eyes flared in anger, but Brother Jacob still had him restrained by the wrist.

"Robin, go get some help to take Eddy to the infirmary," directed Brother Jacob.

I didn't want to leave Eddy alone with these two for long, so I ran to the change room and got three other boys to help.

When I returned, Brother Jacob was standing over Eddy. Brother Rene was nowhere to be seen. I got a sinking feeling when I made eye contact with Brother Jacob. His look made it clear that I was in his debt.

Brother Alvin came close to hysteria when he saw Eddy.

"Who did this?" he screamed.

"Brother Rene," I told him quietly.

Brother Alvin stormed out and came back a few minutes later with the director.

"No doubt the boy asked for it. Just fix him up, Brother Alvin, and I will talk to Brother Rene," said Brother Gordon, after surveying the situation.

"Fix him up!" shrieked Brother Alvin. "Fix him up! There is more fixing here than I can do."

Brother Alvin did his best, but Eddy was concussed and had several broken bones. He went to the hospital and came back with a cast on his right hand and left arm. They had bandaged up his broken ribs and cleaned the gash on his head.

Later, Eddy told me that the people at the hospital were told that he had fallen out of a tree.

Brother Alvin let me stay with Eddy for a while that night. Eddy didn't talk very much; he just listened to me in a tirade while I made big threats and promises of revenge. I felt so helpless and guilty about not being able to prevent the situation in the first place.

Brother Alvin was sadly quiet and just sat in his chair when he wasn't fussing over Eddy. His face was drawn and gray. There was no trace of his usual cheerful countenance. It seemed that he was aging quickly before my eyes. At that moment, I added to my list of things that needed avenging. There was a price to be paid for Brother Alvin's grief.

The next day, I saw the director talking to Brothers Jacob and Rene in the hall. The three of them were laughing happily over some joke or other. I couldn't understand why Rene was still holding court with the director, while Eddy was barely able to move. My anger was now percolating at full boil. I wanted justice. I wanted to hurt them. I wanted them to suffer. No amount of pain would be too severe. I vowed to myself that I would see them writhe in pain and agony, and for a moment, I hoped there was a God, for when I had finished with them, and they were dead, God would send them directly to a burning hell.

It was eight days before Eddy came back to the kitchen. During that time, I had formulated a plan of attack on those sadistic bastards. Eddy had a cast on one arm and a cast on the opposite hand. He obviously wouldn't be much help in the kitchen, but we were all glad to see him. There were shouts of welcome as he entered the kitchen. Eddy smiled weakly as he limped in, wincing with pain every step of the way.

"Eddy, we have a plan to get those fuckers."

Eddy didn't seem too interested at first. It was as if the fight had gone out of him.

"You know," I continued, not wanting him to give in without a contest, "Every day that you were gone, we pissed in the soup—all of us! I got smart however, and put all of the soup in bowls, even the ones without the piss. We put a little salt on the edge of the three bowls without the added ingredient and served them to Brothers Alvin, Beacon and Stephen, so that they wouldn't be seen to have special treatment every day."

Peeing in the soup didn't seem to have any ill effects on the brothers, and the act of pissing in it was one more of contempt, than having any hope of making them ill.

Eddy's smile crept weakly into his eyes, then it lit up his face as he thought about it. I knew I was feeding his anger, but I somehow felt anger was better than lassitude. I felt that our anger and hatred were necessary for our survival. Too many of the boys had given way to submission, and you could see the deadness in their eyes. Some were walking zombies. Others took their anger out on their peers, having a better chance of surviving conflict with the protection of whatever brother had made them their slave.

"Today, in celebration of your return," I said gleefully, "We have a special treat for those bastards. Today, we don't piss in the soup. Today, we have stew!"

He looked at me questioningly; then the light finally dawned on him, and he said, "No! No! No!"

"Too late," I interrupted. "The stew is cooking and three of us have already *shit* in it! Don't worry we stirred it really well and put in a *lot* of spice. They will never know."

We had forgotten, in our full-blown hatred, to take some out for the three brothers that we did not want to harm. We finally decided to give them grilled cheese sandwiches and tell them that the stew would be too spicy for them. I felt Brother Alvin had not given us away to the others.

When I served the brothers, only one of them asked why Brothers Beacon, Alvin and Stephen were getting special orders. I said blandly that they had trouble with spicy foods and that the stew was a bit hot. This seemed to satisfy Brother Beacon, but Brother Alvin scowled at me and said nothing. Brother Stephen, who probably didn't have a stomach problem, looked knowingly at me but said, "Yes, I have been having some serious heartburn. I asked the boys what the ingredients were in the soup and asked if they could give me something a little blander." He looked at Brother Alvin and smiled. "I told them to add you because I know you sometimes have indigestion."

This quite surprised me, and I wondered if Brother Alvin had told him of the previous incident.

Brother Alvin looked at him suspiciously, but said nothing; he looked into my eyes, and I smiled at him. His face became a greenish shade, and he ran from the lunchroom.

Brother Stephen said, "I guess his indigestion is worse than I thought."

"I will go and check and see if he is all right," I volunteered.

"No, you stay here, and do your chores," said Brother Stephen. "I will check on Brother Alvin." He got up from his chair and left the room.

I hurried back into the kitchen, and we destroyed all the evidence of what we thought might be attempted murder.

"Robin Le Blanc, report to Brother Alvin in the infirmary as soon as possible," came the call over the intercom.

When I walked into the infirmary, I could see that Brother Alvin was very angry. His face was still that funny shade of green.

"What was in the stew?" he asked between gritted teeth.

"The time has come for us to get our revenge. Revenge for Eddy, revenge for the little kids, and revenge for me. Me! Me!" I said with vehemence. "I'm fighting back. We all are." I could feel my face twist in hatred, anger making my blood rush to my face.

He stared at me in disillusioned amazement. I sat on the cot, and we looked at each other. I said softly, with a wicked grin on my face, "I shit in the stew."

He was no longer green. Brother Alvin lost all the color in his face. He seemed to have also lost his power of speech. For about two minutes, he said nothing, and I waited.

"You can't be . . . No, say this is not true. My god, are you mad? What have you done?" he sputtered finally.

We stared at each other for another minute.

"I told you, I . . . *shit* . . . in . . ."

"You couldn't have," he interrupted. "I mean, this is unbelievable. How could you?"

I sat there and smiled evilly at him. "I could. I did. I loved it. Every moment."

"Are you happy now?" he asked.

"Yes! Yes! Yes!" I said gleefully.

He stared at me then down at the floor.

"Uncle Alvin?" I asked with some anxiety over his lack of words.

"Why do you call me Uncle Alvin?" He looked into my face, confused at this form of address. I hadn't realized that I had said out loud what seemed natural and fitting, but the name seemed to suit the relationship.

"I guess because you are good, and brother doesn't mean that to me. No," I pondered, "You are the best, you care about us and love us, and I feel safe with you. You are kind. About the stew," I continued, "Brother Marcus said, and I quote, 'Yum, Yum,' so it must have tasted good."

This seemed to make Brother Alvin smile. His smile grew, and there was a rumbling in his throat, as a laugh could no longer stay down, erupting like a volcano from his belly.

He laughed and laughed.

I laughed and laughed.

He stood up and held his side, the tears flowing like rivers down his old, rutted cheeks. A puddle of piss was growing on the floor beneath his robe. Still, we laughed. He slipped and fell in the piss on the floor, landing on his backside. In my attempt to help him up, I fell on the floor beside him, and we looked at each other.

"Yum, Yum," I said, and we laughed even harder.

He grabbed me around the neck and kissed me on the cheek. I reared automatically, looked at him then relaxed, realizing who it was.

His smile died on his face, and he broke into tears.

"I'm sorry. I'm so sorry . . . I didn't mean anything."

"Uncle Alvin, I know the difference. It was just an automatic reaction," I said feeling bad for his anguish. I put my arm around his neck and kissed his cheek.

We helped each other up.

"I didn't mean to upset you, knowing what you have been through." He kept apologizing over and over.

"It's okay," I hugged him harder and said, "I know that you didn't mean it that way."

After an awkward silence, he laughed and said, "I think a shower is in order. You had better go to your dorm and change your clothes and shower."

Following his instructions, I went to the shower room. For once the shower was empty and there was no sign of Brothers Rene or Jacob.

I was standing under the stream of hot water when I felt a hand on my ass. I jumped and turned to find Brother Jacob standing naked, penis erect and wearing only a sly grin.

I panicked and screamed, "Get out! Get out!"

"You owe me, remember?" he leered. "Eddy?"

"It was your duty," I screamed. "Brother Rene was going to kill him!"

"All I want if for us to be lovers. No one need to know, and no one will hurt you or your friend Eddy again," Jacob said this quietly and without agitation.

I looked at him with all the hatred and revulsion burning in my eyes. "Never! You piece of shit!"

Brother Jacob punched me five or six times, then picked up his robe, and left me alone.

I sat on the floor of the shower, the water still running, my nose and mouth bleeding, the blood running down my chest, over my thighs and down the drain. I stayed there for a long time, screaming inside.

"Why, Mom? Why don't you come and get us out from this hell?"

At that moment, I hated her. There was a searing pain at the base of my throat, which seemed to have closed, and I couldn't breathe. It was as though I was being ripped from there to my abdomen.

When the bleeding stopped I got out and dressed and went down to the gym. Eddy walked over and looked at my face for a long moment, my anguish clearly visible.

"Where have you been?" he asked. "What did Brother Alvin do to you? What did you tell him? I have been in a panic since you left. I can tell something bad happened."

Just then, Brother Jacob came into the gym looking very angry. He stopped and glared at me.

"Did he rape you?" Eddy asked in a whisper as if it were an everyday thing. What am I saying? It was an everyday thing in this place.

"No, but he beat me again," I laughed and put on some false bravado. "The fucker can't take no for an answer."

Then I laughed in earnest looking over at Jacob. "It don't hurt, you asshole." And strangely it didn't anymore. I was getting tougher every day, and each beating only made me more callused.

19

The next three hockey games, Eddy and I just went through the motions of playing. We threw the games. Brothers Jacob and Rene were livid.

The whole team was ordered to stand at the wall of the gym for four hours. We were not allowed to eat, drink, or go to the bathroom.

The punishment from these two was always fresh in our minds, and we did not think of disobeying this order. Two of the boys pissed their pants in silence. The next game, none of the regular team was allowed to play. Brother Rene and Brother Jacob used all new players. *Big mistake*. They had had no practice or experience, and they got clobbered. Although the regular team was not allowed to play, we had to watch the game and go to the gym afterward.

Brother Rene came into the gym and slapped each of us in the face. "You will play the next game, and you will win the next game. If you do not win, you will receive far worse than a slap in the face."

We played the next game and won. It was a joyless victory however. The gym was silent as we took off our gear. The dressing room was a morgue. This did not bother our jailers; their threats had worked, and they had total control of us. They congratulated each other about how successfully their threats had worked.

At practice one day, I took a slap shot and connected with Brother Jacob's ankle. He fell on the ice, and I skated over to see if he was all right.

"I'm sorry, Brother Jacob," I said with feigned sincerity. I then skated back toward Eddy smirking. "How do you like that, asshole?" I said to myself.

For the next three days, Brother Jacob limped, and it felt good to see him on the receiving end of pain. Eddy thought it was very funny. Brother Jacob, of course, assumed the shot had been intentional, and I knew that at some point he would retaliate.

During our next game, the opposite team scored the first goal. I smiled at Eddy and said, "Okay, one for them. Now we will take the next three." We both laughed.

Brother Jacob observed us laughing and called me over to the bench. "Sit down," he said.

As I sat down, he grabbed a handful of my hair at the back of my head and punched me in the face. I heard a crunch and felt excruciating pain in my nose. Blood was poring out of my nostrils and down my chin.

"Do you think this is funny too? Why aren't you laughing now? Huh? Smart ass. Losing games is getting to be a habit with you." He was hollering and ranting. "Now go back to the gym and stand against the wall. I will deal with you later."

After the game, Brother Jacob came up to me in the gym and said, "You will stand here until I tell you otherwise."

When I thought everyone had gone, Eddy came in and handed me a wet towel. I wiped my face and nose. It had stopped bleeding, but hurt like hell.

I spent the night in the gym, and in the morning, Brother Jacob told me that I could continue to stand there until it was time for class. I was not allowed any breakfast.

My face was a swollen mess when I went to class, and it was obvious to Brother Stephen that I was exhausted when I went to class.

"What happened to you, Robin?" he asked.

I told him what had happened, and he said, "Put your head down on your desk, and I will wake you when the class is over."

When he woke me, he brought some fruit and a donut. I was having trouble breathing and found it hard to swallow, but the food felt good in my stomach even though I had trouble tasting it.

"Now don't tell anyone that I did this, or I will be the one standing against the wall next!" he joked.

We went to the gym to line up for lunch, and Brother Jacob came to me and said, "There will be no lunch for you, and you can stand against the wall during lunch."

The brothers' lunchroom entrance was off the gym. I saw Brother Stephen and Brother Alvin talking, as they entered the lunchroom. Brother Alvin came back out to me with a salt shaker and said, "Go and fill this for me," and then he lowered his voice "Grab something to eat and don't get caught!" Both Brother Jacob and Brother Rene were overseeing the boys' lunchroom.

I went to the kitchen with the salt shaker and grabbed a piece of bread. Eddy gave me a hunk of baloney, and I bolted it down. I took the salt shaker into the lunchroom and sat it down in front of Uncle Alvin. As I set it down in front of him I bent over and gave him a kiss on the cheek.

Brother Alvin blushed. "Get out of here before you get caught," he said.

I went back to the gym. After lunch, Eddy came and stood in front of me. "I brought you some cookies," he said as he pulled several out of his pocket. With Eddy covering me, I devoured the cookies gratefully.

Not long after that Brother Jacob came over to me and said, "If you think that you have learned your lesson now, you can go with the others."

"Yes, Brother Jacob," I said humbly, "Thank you."

I certainly was learning lots of lessons in this place. I was learning to hate with religious fervor.

20

There were a lot of boys on the junior side. I knew some of my brothers' friends to see them, but we had our own groups, and I didn't know many of the little kids.

Some of the little boys, from five to seven, didn't fare very well. They would cry themselves to sleep and didn't have many social skills. There was one small boy in Paul's group. He was very shy and seemed to have adopted Paul. His name was Michael. He stuck to Paul like a moss. He had huge blue eyes and white, blond hair. Paul seemed to get used to him and looked out for him if the others were taunting him.

Paul was changing. Not too long before he had stuck to me in the same manner, and now he was the protector. He seemed to have taken on the role of leader with his peer group.

Along with that role, he also got more unwanted attention from the brothers. He seemed to be able to hold his own though, and I now wondered if he suffered the same abuses as I. He stopped telling me everything that happened to him, and at the time, I was so wrapped up in my own life, I didn't notice. Even then I realized that, when we finally got out, we would probably not speak of the atrocities inflicted on us. Neither of us would ever admit to being victims.

One day, Paul came to the kitchen door and called to me. We were just in the middle of preparing a no-surprise supper.

I went over to the door, "What's wrong?" I asked.

"It's Michael," he said. "I can't find him anywhere."

"Did you look in the gym? The washroom? The library? Is he with your teacher?" I queried.

Paul kept shaking his head.

"Did one of the brothers take him somewhere? Was he being punished?" I continued.

"I don't know. He was with me when we left class, and I went to the washroom, and he was gone. No one has seen him." Paul looked very worried as he said this.

I didn't feel too concerned, and I had to get back to my chores. "Maybe he has just gone off somewhere to be by himself," I suggested half-heartedly, not really believing it. One thing there was a shortage of were places to hide; I knew, I had often tried to find one.

Paul was miserable. "Keep looking," I said. "I will help you after supper."

When we were in the dining room serving dinner, Paul came up to fill his plate with Michael in tow. Paul was very relieved. I looked at Michael, whose head was down, and he had red welts on his cheeks. He was crying silently.

"Look after him, Paul," I advised my brother.

Michael's hands shook as he handed me his plate—another lost soul.

I couldn't dwell on it too long as I went about my chores. I saw them again later in the gym. Paul was holding court with his peers, Michael firmly positioned as close to Paul's side as possible without clinging to him.

I looked around for my two archenemies. They were over in a corner and didn't seem to pay the slightest attention to the group of little kids. In fact, in spite of Paul getting a little more attention from the brothers, Paul's group was usually left alone. They had learned the art of being wallpaper.

I didn't know much about Michael except that he had no parents and had been in foster homes from birth until he came to the school.

I was very proud of Paul. He had been my biggest worry when we had arrived at the school. He was so little and vulnerable, and now he seemed to have found a way of coping. He had his own group of friends and, unlike me, had maintained some sensitivity and gentleness toward others. Mom would be proud of him, I thought. I quickly admonished myself for thinking that Mom would give a damn. Never mind, I was proud of him.

I watched Michael for a bit. His eyes were glassy, and he had pulled into himself. He moved whenever Paul did keeping within a couple of inches of Paul at all times.

21

Before the wake-up bell in the morning, I was awakened by the sound of one of the boys talking hysterically to Brother Jacob.

"It's Michael. He isn't breathing. His eyes are open and there is blood everywhere!"

Brother Jacob hurried to Michael's bed and looked at him, turned on his heel and scurried out. I was afraid to look at Michael. Brother Jacob came back with the director, Uncle Alvin, Brother Stephen, Brother Beacon and Brother Mark. Brother Mark taught in the English side, and we didn't have too much to do with him. I had seen him take rounds out of boys in the grounds, and he could be just as cruel as Brothers Rene and Jacob. Sometimes in the free time, when both groups of boys were together in the gym, he would be supervising there as well.

They all hurried to Michael's bed. Shock registered on their faces. The boy who had found Michael was still fixed to the spot. The director noticed him, turned him around and aimed him toward his bed.

The director then announced loudly, "Everyone get up and go to the gym. Do not get dressed, just go to the gym and wait. Now!"

I spotted Paul. He was moving like a zombie. I went back and took his arm and dragged him down the stairs with me.

Once our confused assembly reached the gym, we all spoke in whispers, as one does at a funeral home. The word *dead* was rumbling in my mind, and then I heard it move through the gym like a flashflood, rolling over everything in its path.

We watched out the windows, expecting an ambulance, or a police car, or a hearse, or all of these things. Soon after, we had arrived at the school, one of the older brothers had died, and a hearse came for his body. That day, no vehicle arrived—front or back.

We were in the gym in our underwear for a long time. It was a strange and eerie place. Never had this many unsupervised boys all been in one spot and so quiet.

Eventually, the director came down and told us to get dressed. Eddy and I should have started breakfast by now, and the director told us just to put out some cold cereal and not to bother making porridge.

When we went up to the dorm, we cast surreptitious glances toward the spot where Michael's cot had been. It was gone. The beds in that row had been moved so that there was no gap where his had stood. It was like we had dreamed the whole thing—even Michael's very existence.

In class, Brother Stephen looked drawn and tired, but he did not allude to the incident. We waited to be given the explanation that did not come, and none of us had the nerve to ask.

He assigned chapters to read in our history books, not bothering to instruct us. He stared down at the open book on his desk with unfocused eyes. Of course, no one could concentrate on reading, but it was the quietest and longest class I had ever sat through.

Eddy and I left early to start lunch. We were out in the hall, and he whispered, "What happened?"

"I don't know, but you can bet your ass that we aren't going to see Michael again," I said.

"But where did he go? What can they have done with him?" Eddy persisted.

I shrugged. I wanted to know the same things. I kept thinking of those two bloated octopuses in the basement with fire enough to make quick work of bones and flesh. I tried to erase this horror from my mind and didn't speak the thought aloud. If I voiced this thought, the whole nightmare I had been living would have taken on so much evil that I was sure I wouldn't recover—ever.

Eddy kept pestering me with questions and speculation; I felt a cold core growing in my gut. I didn't feel like talking. Fear and shock now took on a new definition and magnitude, and the words seemed to be too small for the cold rock that had settled in my abdomen.

I didn't want to think. It was dawning on me that the walls of this school were impenetrable to the law. I was sure that at least one of the brothers was responsible, and the rest were covering. They would cover up murder to protect their holy order.

When I went into the brothers' dining room, I looked for Uncle Alvin. I thought that I would get some answers just by the look on his face. He was not there. I had a glimmer of hope that Michael was in the infirmary, and Uncle Alvin was looking after him. I went back to the kitchen and asked Eddy to cover for me while I ran up to the infirmary.

I got as far as the bottom of the stairs, and Rene came out of the dining room. "Le Blanc, where are you going?"

Shit.

"Err . . . I was just going to see if Unc . . . er . . . Brother Alvin wanted some lunch," I ad-libbed.

"He isn't up there," said Brother Rene, not offering any explanation.

I looked at his face and for once he didn't have that angry, mean expression. Instead, he wore an expression of fear, shock, and sadness. It seemed to be the reflection of all that I was feeling.

Eddy approached me as I reentered the kitchen. "Well?" he asked.

"Nothing. Brother Rene stopped me. He said Uncle Alvin isn't up there." I really didn't feel like talking, not even to Eddy.

The remainder of the day dragged. Supper prep was quiet; Eddy eventually seemed to sense that I didn't want to talk. Finally, free time came, and I sought out Paul. He was standing by himself in a corner, just staring at nothing.

"Hey," I said with a forced smile. "How is it going?"

He looked up at me, tears welling in his eyes. "What happened? I don't understand. I need to understand."

"Shhh," I said, looking around.

"I don't know, but it can't be good. Nobody is talking," I whispered.

The brothers were huddled on the far side of the room, not talking to each other or even looking at each other, and ignoring all of us.

Paul seemed to have transformed from child to angry animal. He looked at me and said, "We don't have any choices. We can all be killed in our beds, and no one in the world would know."

I was surprised as he echoed my thoughts. He was too young to think like this.

Peter approached us. I hadn't seen him all day. He had become withdrawn since we arrived at the school. He didn't make friends, and he wasn't involved in sports. He just seemed to go where he was led like a timid sheep. He had made himself invisible, and never had any attention focused on him. He didn't say anything. He just stood there expecting to be told what to do and how to react. I felt a surge of unfair anger directed toward him.

"Stay with Paul," I snapped. I should have been able to entrust him with Paul's care, but probably the roles would be reversed.

Peter still didn't speak, and I didn't have time to worry about him. I went to Eddy and asked if he had seen Uncle Alvin.

"No, and every time anyone goes near the stairs, the bastards make them come back into the gym," said Eddy.

Brother Stephen was standing apart from the other Brothers like a mute statue. I thought about going over to talk to him, but there was something prohibitive in his manner that stopped me.

For days, we waited to hear something. Nothing was said. Eventually, things returned to normal, and Uncle Alvin was back, looking older and sadder. (Uncle Alvin told us that he had gone on a sabbatical at a retreat for brothers and priests.)

The incident of Michael's death numbed me; all my beliefs had been shattered to the foundation. Life meant nothing. By now, we were all sure that Michael was dead. There would be no family to investigate, because he had none. One or more of the brothers were responsible, but they seemed to be looking at each other in speculation, and I was convinced that, except for the culprit(s), the others didn't know who had been the author of this heinous crime.

None of the brothers seemed to be able to look Uncle Alvin in the eye, and he had removed himself from them. He spent a lot of time with the little kids. They clung to him like a life raft. He had taken to reading Bible stories to them in the evenings. He would sit on a chair, and the little ones sat on the floor in front of him, listening to his gentle voice, letting it work its healing balm on their frightened souls. Two or three of the smaller boys would cling to his legs as he read. Uncle Alvin would reach down and pat them on the head and smile sadly at their adoring, dependent faces. He seemed to be nursing his own pain as well as theirs. The brothers gave him a wide berth allowing him to work his magic.

Peter joined in with the smaller kids and Paul withdrew. Paul left his peers behind. He became withdrawn and angry. He snapped at his former friends until they deserted him. I couldn't get through to him and eventually he even shunned me, as if blaming me for being unable to prevent the situation.

22

Letters from home were sporadic, and we could never write the truth in our letters.

Any letters we wrote were given unsealed to the director, and he would censor any negative news going out. We could not report abuses or even any unhappiness. Our letters could only relay things about classes and sports and portray a positive picture of the school.

We received several newsy letters from Crystal and John. They had been successful in their adoption of Mary and were very excited about this. Their aunt and uncle in Toronto had taken in Julie and Mark, and I guess that it was a good thing. It would be a big change for them from the outskirts of nowhere to the big city. Pierre was still staying with them until the end of the school year. He had been accepted in an apprenticeship program to become a mechanic. He would start working in Fort St. Luke in the summer.

I did write them a couple of times, but gave up writing letters very early because there seemed to be little point to them. The rules made it a waste of time, and all I wanted to do was tell the truth of what was happening to me and all the other boys in the school. I didn't want to write to my mother and make her feel good about us being here, allowing her to justify her actions or lack thereof. I now felt that even if I could get word out, I wouldn't be believed. I wasn't even sure that *I* believed all that had happened.

As the months went by, home became more and more remote. I had become institutionalized. What had originally shocked and sickened me had become such ordinary, everyday occurrences that I became hardened to them. Sometimes, I didn't even see them. This place had become home, and I was no longer the child who had entered these doors just a few months ago.

It is like moving to a different country and culture. Gradually I was learning the ways of this place. I knew what actions would create specific responses and punishments. I knew that I had to keep my back to the wall and be on guard at all times. Much like a child learns that caution is needed when crossing the road or being too near to an open flame. I was learning caution in areas that no child should even have had to be aware. I was definitely being rehabilitated.

In that short time, I had learned to shun and hate authority, since all authority seemed to take away human rights. Authority represented the evils of mankind, and seemed to be counter to good. Those in control must be fought every step of the way, and then squashed.

One day, I found Uncle Alvin in his rocking chair comforting a small boy. The boy's nose had been broken, and I don't know who looked more upset—`Uncle Alvin or the boy.

Uncle Alvin looked up at me as I entered, tears running down the deep chasms of his cheeks. He seemed unable to speak and just pointed down at the boy. I waited a few minutes before saying anything, and Uncle Alvin, who stood and carried the boy to the bed and put him down. He closed the door of the infirmary.

"You have to do something," I said, feeling a great urgency.

"We have to do something," I amended.

"I can't," he said simply.

"You are a coward," I said in disgust. As soon as the words were out of my mouth, I regretted them. The hurt on his face at that moment still haunts me.

"You don't understand," he sighed. "I have taken a vow. I promised never to say anything that would embarrass the Catholic Church or make it look bad."

Brother Alvin was just about five feet tall and couldn't have weighed more than one hundred pounds. He was around sixty years old and had more love and kindness in him than anyone I had ever known. His convictions toward his God and his religion were unshakable. He never swayed from his beliefs, even when his faith in humanity was destroyed.

23

During the winter, Brother Stephen posted a notice on the bulletin board. There was to be a math contest, and the two boys with the best marks from each grade would be taken on a trip for the weekend to Montreal. There they would be taken to the forum to watch a hockey game between Montreal and Detroit.

Brother Stephen would be testing the French-speaking boys.

Peter entered the contest without much hope of winning. He was pretty awful at math, but his hunger to go was so strong that I wanted him to win even more than he did. It was one of the few times he had shown any interest in anything since we had arrived. He lacked animation to such a degree that I thought that he would never get over our stay here. If he could win this contest, maybe he would begin to show an interest in other things as well. Maybe he would be able to take one good thing from here if we ever got out.

I seemed to have the kind of mind that found math logical, and even though I was only in grade six, I was already working on grade-eight math. I knew that I would win a place on the trip, but it was even more important to me that my brother should win.

Not everyone entered the contest, and we were all tested in one room. I sat behind my brother, and when I had finished my own test, I whispered to him to pass his test to me. I then did his test as well and slipped it back to him. Only Brother Stephen was overseeing the test room, and he stayed at the front. We were at the back, and he didn't catch us.

Brother Stephen collected the tests, and we waited for him to mark them. When he was done, he looked up from his task, and his face was flushed with anger.

He said that he would have to spend some more time marking the tests, and we would be informed of the winners later in the day. He then asked me and Peter to stay back.

"It seems that we have a budding genius in grade four," he said.

He then called my brother up to the front of the room and put three math questions on the board. "Now please show me how to solve these problems, young man," Brother Stephen said to Peter.

Peter's face was scarlet as he demonstrated that he didn't have a clue where to begin and was unable to solve any of them.

I slunk down in my seat, hoping that some act of God would stop the inevitable from happening.

"Robin, maybe you could come up and show your brother how it is done," called Brother Stephen.

I went slowly to the board and took the chalk from my brother. Once there, it didn't occur to me to get the questions wrong. I liked math problems, and these were so easy for me that I just did them. I liked more challenging problems and would often find them a good diversion from the now-normal desperate thoughts I had. Often, I put myself to sleep trying to solve some problem or other.

When I had completed the problems correctly, Brother Stephen said, "They should be right, since you did the test for your brother, and the score on that test was perfect. You did do that didn't you, Robin?" Brother Stephen looked down at me in disappointed sadness.

"Yes," I said, hanging my head in shame.

Brother Stephen walked around the desk and opened the drawer. He extracted a large strap and said, "Hold out your hands." He seemed less angry than frustrated.

I did as I was told resignedly and received ten whacks on each hand.

"You realize, Robin, that both of the tests—yours and your brother's—will be voided, and you are disqualified for cheating," he said sadly. "Return to your seat, and I want to talk to you."

Brother Stephen told Peter he could return to his regular activities.

Brother Stephen sat in the desk next to mine and asked, "Why, Robin? Why would you do that? It isn't like you to cheat."

I began to cry. "My brother never gets to do anything or go anywhere. I have friends, hockey and sports, and he seems to have nothing. He really wanted to go, and it would have made me feel good to help him get there." I sobbed and wiped my nose on my sleeve.

I not only felt protective toward my brothers, I felt responsible for every aspect of their lives. I had become their surrogate parent.

"If you had come to me and told me, I could have sent him instead of you. It was a sure thing that you would have won a seat on the trip." Brother Stephen shook his head. "Cheating is wrong, no matter what the reason. I thought you would have more respect for yourself and have more faith in me."

Shit.

I felt worse about letting Brother Stephen down than all the beatings I had received so far. It cut me deeply, and for once, I was truly sorry for my actions.

I apologized, tears streaming down my face, and I promised never to cheat again.

Brother Stephen did not report the incident to any higher authority, and he somehow arranged for Peter to go on the trip to Montreal.

I thanked him over and over and told him, "You are the greatest! You never punish anyone unless they deserve it, like I did. Peter didn't want me to cheat, but I thought I knew best."

Brother Stephen blushed and turned away.

When Peter came back from the trip, he was on cloud nine. His pleasure gave me great satisfaction, and I felt that I had been partly responsible for his momentary happiness. It seemed that there was still a small part of me that wasn't cold and callused.

I told Peter to thank Brother Stephen and apologize.

Peter said, "Why should I apologize? I wasn't the one who wanted to cheat on the test. I could have had your place without cheating because you were sure to win."

I looked in amazement at him. There was nothing to say. I didn't even feel angry or hurt—just numb.

Peter did, however, thank Brother Stephen. Later he told me that he had told Brother Stephen he was the greatest, and Brother Stephen had accused him of talking too much to his brother.

24

Spring arrived, and the earth became pregnant with new life, and the sap began to move in the maples. Maple syrup time was here, and with it came *hope*—Mother Nature's springtime mate. The mixture worked its delusional drug on all. I could feel new life burst as we were given different tasks in the bush. All the boys were expected to work in the bush, and most would have been very upset if they had not been given a chance to work with the syrup.

There was an old Clydesdale horse that worked pulling a wagon up and down the hill, to and from the sugar bush. Hoses ran between the trees. Spigots were tapped into each tree, and hoses were attached to the spout of the taps. The sap would run through the hose and into large barrels that were set on one of the two wagons. The horse would be hooked to the wagon once the barrels were full, and he would take the wagon down the hill to the perpetually burning fire at the bottom. Two great cauldrons would hang over the fire, and the sap was siphoned into the cauldrons. There it would bubble away until it turned into wonderful maple syrup. Hot syrup would be poured on the melting snow, and when it solidified, we would all be given some to eat. It is not a taste that has ever been duplicated for me in all these years, although I have had the process repeated. Something in the taste buds must be lost with age.

I seemed to be able to lose myself in the bush during that time. I enjoyed the new life that was bursting out of the earth. Mushrooms and fungus would sprout on and around the base of the trees. The robins were breaking the trail for the tardier birds. Once I learned what my chore in the bush was, I would go about doing it, blocking everyone and everything else out.

My first job had been to make sure that the hoses were properly attached to the spigots on the trees and check for any splits in the hoses. One job I had was to siphon the sap from the barrels on the wagon into the cauldrons. My favorite job was the time they let me take the reins and take the wagon up and down the hill.

Most of the syrup was bottled and sold with the crest of the school on the front of the bottle. It was a big money maker, but some was kept aside for the school, and we would have it on Shrove Tuesday, and special Sundays with pancakes or French toast.

I could feel a healing, and I felt hopeful and positive about life once again, almost like I had felt about life once a long time ago at that all but forgotten place called home.

Maple syrup time was too short, and I wanted to cling to it forever. Like all wonderful things in life, they are only remembered as wonderful because of their rarity, and the opportunity to become bored with them through familiarity, has never been an option. Even my feelings of resentment and need for revenge disappeared during the time in the bush.

All too soon we had to return to the regular routine and back indoors. Perhaps because of the confinement inflicted upon me in those dark times, I find indoors unbearable most of the time. Even now, I only spend time there to eat and sleep, no matter what the weather.

25

There was always competition of some sort at the school, pitting boys against boys, as well as boys against the brothers. One such competition involved a math contest that put the English-speaking boys against the French-speaking boys. I was picked to represent the French-speaking grades six to eight class in the contest. The day before the contest, Brother Stephen told me to not bother with anything but studying my math.

"You will have to be your sharpest tomorrow, Robin. We are all counting on you," he said. "Make sure you know how to do all the problems in the grade-eight book especially. Get a good night's sleep as well."

I was anxious that I do well to make up for the disappointment I had caused Brother Stephen over the test incident.

There were four on our team. One boy representing grade four, one grade five, one for grade nine, and me for grades six to eight.

The English team had six members—one kid for each grade. The English master queried this. When he was informed that I was in grade six, and not in grade eight, he could not complain about us having an advantage. He was also told that the director had given his approval for me to represent the three grades, and he had no grounds for complaint.

Brother Mark was the English schoolmaster. I had never had any personal dealings with him. I had seen his cruelty to the kids he supervised and wondered if he was as competitive as Brothers Jacob and Rene. If he was I felt sorry for his team, since I fully intended to win the match.

The contest took place in the large meeting hall. The whole school assembled to watch and cheer their side on.

On the stage, tables were set up for the contestants, one for each team. There was a blackboard set on an easel on which the questions were written, one at a time. Names were taped on the desk in front of each contestant.

The director began the contest saying, "We will begin with the grade four representatives."

He then explained, "There will be twenty questions for each grade. The questions will be written on the board one at a time. The boy answering each question first will be given a point for his team. The person with the most correctly answered questions will be the winner of the round. The team that wins the most rounds will be the champions. Each contestant will be given paper and pencil in order to work out answers."

He sat down, and the games began. Our grade four representative lost the first round by one question.

The cheers on the English side of the assembly hall were deafening.

The grade-five contestant lost his round as well. The English were on their feet applauding and yelling. The French kids were mute and glum.

I had been fairly confident until then, thinking that our team would beat them hands down. I waited nervously for my turn, and when it came I won the round for the grade-six competition by five points. I did expect this since I had moved past this point in math easily. The grade seven questions were still easy, and I had no problem taking the round. The grade eight questions became a little more difficult, and after sixteen questions, we were tied. I won the seventeenth and eighteenth questions, and he won the nineteenth and twentieth.

There was a tie-breaking question, and I could feel the perspiration on my brow. The sweat poured under my arms. The question was more difficult and after a minute, I was sure the other kid would beat me to the answer. I glanced at his face and saw that he was struggling too. Finally, I saw the answer and shouted it out without raising my hand. The director raised his eyebrow, and I realized what I had done and raised my hand. He hesitated before acknowledging me, and for a minute, I thought he would wait for my opponent to come up with the answer. I answered it correctly, then realized that I had won by one question. I flushed with success and had enjoyed an even contest.

Our grade nine representative won his round but the decision had to be made with twenty-one questions again to break the tie.

The French boys were jumping up and down and yelling to beat the band. "Three cheers for our side," shouted Brother Stephen over the din.

I looked down and saw Brother Mark glowering directly at me.

26

About a week after the math contest, Brother Mark came to our classroom and asked Brother Stephen if he could use me to show his class how to do the math problem that was the last question I answered in the contest.

Brother Stephen said, "Sure. Robin, go with Brother Mark and do as he instructs."

As we walked down the hall to the other classroom, Brother Mark said, "I want you to show my class how smart you really are."

I looked up at him, not sure what he was saying, but realized that he did not mean this to be complimentary.

Once in the classroom, Brother Mark addressed the kids in his class, "Okay, boys, Frenchie here will show you how it's done."

He turned to me, "Right, Frenchie?"

"My name is Robin," I said in English, looking him straight in the eye. "Not Frenchie."

"Not only are you smart, you have a smart mouth as well," he glared at me and punched me in the side of the jaw. I fell to the floor dazed. Brother Mark was about six feet, two inches tall and weighed around 230 pounds.

I attempted to get up, and he kicked me in the side. The classroom was very quiet.

"Tough too, eh?" he sneered.

I couldn't breathe, and I thought I would choke to death. He picked me up and threw me into the hall.

"Now fuck off, Frenchie, and don't come back!" he screamed and slammed the door.

I staggered back to my classroom in a daze. Brother Stephen jumped up and grabbed me before I fell into the doorway. "What happened?" he asked in a panic.

"Brother Mark beat the crap out of me, that's what happened," I said.

Brother Stephen's anger was visible, and he said, "Come with me."

Brother Stephen was about the same size, although a lot more fit than Brother Mark. He was all muscle, whereas Brother Mark was very flabby. We went back to Brother Mark's room, and Brother Stephen opened the door without knocking.

"Come out here for a minute, Brother Mark," he said quietly.

When Brother Mark came out, Brother Stephen grabbed his hand, and I could see Brother Mark's face twist in pain.

"Don't you *ever*," hissed Brother Stephen through clenched teeth, "Touch one of my boys again. Do you hear me? Pick on someone your own size and then see who comes out the winner."

Brother Mark said nothing.

"Come with me, Robin," said Brother Stephen turning to walk down the hall. I followed but not without turning to see Brother Mark rubbing his hand. I gave him the finger.

Back in class, I thought, "Is there no end to the number of sick bastards in this world, or are they all here?"

The one compensation was that Brother Stephen was on my side, and he was a hero for me.

27

In July, we had police day. On this day, the police arrived in ten or twelve patrol cars and a couple of paddy wagons. The purpose of the day was to establish a good relationship between the boys and the police. The weather was warm and sunny, and perfect for outdoor activities.

There was a barbecue and games. We played baseball and tug-of-war games against the cops. We were taken for rides in the police cars and allowed to turn on the sirens.

When I had a chance, and was alone with one of the policemen, I told him about some of the sadistic things that went on at the school. I realized that this was my chance to maybe change some things and perhaps see the sick bastards get what they deserved. I must have been living in a dream world.

The cop listened to me intently, and I thought he believed me enough to at least investigate. He said he would see what he could do.

Around two thirty in the afternoon, I was talking to Eddy, and told him what I had told the cop. He looked over my shoulder, and his face turned pale.

"Oh, oh," said Eddy. "You are going to get killed."

I turned to see that same cop talking to the director and the director looking over in my direction. They were having a good laugh about something.

"You're dead," Eddy said worriedly.

"Fuck him," I said in resignation.

I should have known! I looked over at the two of them, laughing. Then the director excused himself to the cop and casually walked over to us.

"Oh, shit! Oh, shit!" muttered Eddy as the director approached.

"Robin, I want you to go to my office and wait there for me." He said this without any outward evidence of anger.

I waited in his office for hours. He didn't come until the police had long gone and after supper, around seven in the evening. He came in and sat down at his desk, tidying some papers before he spoke.

"We arranged a wonderful day for you boys, and you decided it was your job to spoil it," he said.

He stood up and reached across the desk and slapped me on the side of the head seven or eight times, and then gave me the old stand-by. I got eight lashes with the strap.

"Now go to your dorm and to bed," he said.

When I got to the dorm, Brother Jacob was waiting for me. "I could have helped you if you weren't so stubborn," he grinned.

"Kiss my ass, you faggot," I responded.

Brother Jacob took his round out of me and left.

I lay there in my bed and decided that enough was enough.

The next day I went to the gym and seriously started working out. I used the punching bag, and as I punched it, I pretended that it was each of the brothers who had abused me. My unprotected hands hurt as I punched and thought of all the assholes holding us hostage and using us for their punching bags.

I caught a glimpse of my reflection at that time, and the face that stared back at me was not the one I knew. I was no longer a child, and I could see stress that should not have existed in my now-thirteen-year-old face. It angered me to have lost my youth; I was an old man in a child's body. My determination to beat them at their own game was only heightened by what I saw.

I ran up and down the stairs, skipped rope, sparred with the air and was in perpetual motion trying to build up muscles and become strong enough to take any of the bastards that came my way. I did this for three weeks, and then Brother Stephen, who had been watching me with interest for quite a while, took me aside.

"I know what you are trying to do, Robin," he said. "You cannot win no matter what, and you are going to get badly hurt. You should give up on the idea of revenge."

"Never," I said. "I don't care if they kill me, but I'm not going to take it anymore without a fight."

Brother Stephen saw the determination on my face. "Then you had better have some proper instruction so that you can do it right and not get too badly hurt. Come to the gym, and we will work together."

He showed me how to box and fight, how to avoid punches and build up my muscle tone. I worked at it whenever I had any spare time. I was driven with hatred. I was like a dog that had been tied and caged. I was meaner and angrier that I would have thought possible a year before. The only thing that stopped me from making an unwarranted attack on the brothers was fear for my own brothers.

28

The library was located on the third floor of the building. We had regular library classes where we were expected to read and give book reports. Brother Hubert, who was an easy-going teacher, ran the class. We laughed a lot in that class, mostly at our peers who were giving a report. Brother Hubert tried to maintain control, but he usually ended up laughing with us.

There were elements in the school that did follow the picture that the institution portrayed to the outside world. There were opportunities to play sports and be trained in those sports; there was a farming operation that taught a lot about farming and animal husbandry; all academic bases were covered; food was adequate and well balanced diets were the norm; the boys were cleanly dressed and bathed; religion was taught in the school; and there were caring brothers.

The other side of the coin, the one unknown to the people who blindly sent kids here, was darker and overshadowed the good that could be done here. In fact, had it not been for the perverted bent of some, those who were given carte-blanche ward ship, the school might have achieved its intended mandate.

The fact that there were no women to bring their nurturing and calming influence to the school was a grave mistake. Not that all women are impervious to the effects of power on their psyche, but they are, as a rule, the more gentle of the species and have a more compassionate nature than men.

Pure testosterone seems to generate violence when not balanced by some estrogen. If women had been part of the supervision and teaching of the boys, there would have been a smidgen of balance and normalcy that exists in the real world. As it was, we rarely saw any female, young or old.

There was a woman from the village, however, who would bring baking for the brothers. She felt that the brothers were modern-day saints, sacrificing their lives for the errant boys who were put away in the school.

She would come through the kitchen and lecture us on how lucky we were to be given the opportunity to be here and the privilege of a second chance. (As opposed to having public floggings and our hands cut off, I supposed.) She made it sound like we had been given a chance to go to a posh camp for free. She also seemed to feel that we were only there through her charity.

We would just keep our heads down, unable to show her the anger in our eyes at these misconceptions. We knew from bitter experience that people believed what they wanted to believe. We had no hope of changing those beliefs, and any attempt would only bring us more painful punishment and serve no useful purpose.

When we were out in the field playing baseball or football, many of the townspeople would come and watch. It must have been like a visit to the zoo. There were quite a few girls who seemed to be drawn to the rebellious youths they must have thought we were.

We were not allowed to fraternize with these temptresses, and if we so much as looked at any of them, we were in for a beating.

One girl, about thirteen years old, would come and watch us play hockey. She and Eddy had somehow managed to talk to each other when there were no brothers watching. They would talk through the chain link fence and touch hands through the holes.

On an afternoon after a game, Eddy leaned his face near the fence, and the girl did the same. They kissed through the fence, and when Eddy tried to pull away, he found that his lips were stuck on the fence.

He was making desperate noises, and I went over to see what had happened. I started to laugh as he made noises through unmoving lips. I didn't know what to do and finally had to go and find help. I told the girl she had better disappear and ran into the building.

The first person I saw was Brother Rene. "Where is your sidekick, Robin?"

I didn't want to tell Brother Rene anything, but I did need to get some help. At the moment, he seemed quite sane, and I didn't know how to go past him without answering him.

"He's stuck. I need some help," I said.

"What do you mean stuck?" asked Brother Rene.

"On the fence," I said, "His lips are stuck on the fence."

Rene looked at me in amazement and headed toward the door. He went up to Eddy and roared with laughter.

"That was a stupid thing to do. Why would you stick your mouth on the fence? Have you no brains at all?" Brother Rene was enjoying himself.

Eddy's eyes moved desperately around, and Rene grabbed him by the hair and yanked him off the fence. Eddy let out a yelp as half of his lip was left on the fence. Rene laughed maniacally as he headed back into the building.

Eddy's lips were bleeding, and he asked, "Why did you get *him*, you prick?"

"I didn't," I said. "He asked where you were, and I told him you were stuck. He just came." I was injured that he would think that I would purposely get Rene to come to his aid. Then I looked at him, and the humor of the situation overcame me, and I started to laugh.

"Yeah, you bastard, laugh," he said and then he smiled. The smile brought on more bleeding, and I couldn't help but laugh harder.

One day, we were all told to get our bathing suits on. We had to go to the pool and search for a two-year-old child that was missing from the village. The brothers thought he might be in the pool. We all went to the pool with feelings of dread. None of us wanted to find the child there.

"I found him!" one of my peers shouted as he pulled the small body to the edge of the pool. There were tears running down his face, knowing that he had just added another thread to the tapestry of the nightmare and pain that would live with him and the rest of us forever, and could be relived nightly in our dreams.

29

I saw Brother Jacob talking to my youngest brother after supper. He took him by the hand and headed up the stairs from the gym. I ran up the stairs and confronted him, standing three steps up from him. I glared at Brother Jacob, and he let go of Paul's hand.

"What do you want, Robin?" he asked.

"You keep your filthy hands off my brother," I said.

"What are you saying? What are you accusing me of?" He asked this in mock innocence. "I will let him go, but only if you will come with me instead."

"Let him go," I repeated.

"Okay, you have made your choice," responded Brother Jacob with a leer.

My brother was released, and I saw over Brother Jacob's shoulder that Paul had run to safety beside Eddy, who now had both of my brothers with him and was trying to lead them away. Paul, however, would not be distracted and watched what was happening on the stairs.

Brother Jacob grabbed me by the sweater and pulled me toward him. "Now you will come with me." We were now both on the same step as he slapped me. I managed to free my sweater, and I started back down the stairs and toward the middle of the gym. Once in the middle, I stopped.

"You want me to love you," I said loudly so that all could hear. "You had me in your room upstairs, and you were naked. You want to make love to me. It would be 'soooo nice,' you told me. We would give each other pleasure. You would look after me, and I would be taken care of. I would then have all the favors and treats that a boy could want," I continued to shout.

The kids all stopped what they were doing to watch this confrontation. There wasn't a sound for about fifteen seconds. Jacob's face was beet-red.

"Come and get me, you bastard," I screamed holding my hands out, beckoning with my fingers. I let all the power of my rage wash over my trembling body. My pulse was pounding in my ears. The hatred I felt had taken over every inch of my body.

"But," I screamed out, "Until death do us part, you fucking piece of shit!"

I jumped toward him and punched him in the face. Stunned only for a moment, he came back laughing. I punched. I kicked. I bit. Brother Jacob's smile disappeared. Every move was countered. The kids were yelling and cheering with every punch I landed.

"Kill the fucker, Robin!" they yelled.

His eye had a mouse. Blood streamed from his nose. His lip was split. A direct hit to my jaw sent me rolling over the pool table. I jumped up on the table and lunged at him. In mid air, a fist met my jaw. I dropped to the floor. Black shoes and the bottom of a robe faced me. Brother Mark had changed the odds. Punches and kicks landed everywhere on my body. I felt one of my teeth break. My nose cracked, jaw crunched, vision blurred, and blood and sweat covered my face.

Eddy ran over to Brother Alvin and yelled, "Help him, you fucking coward!"

Uncle Alvin looked stunned and then grabbed his cane. He jumped over me to protect me from their blows.

"Enough! Enough!" he yelled hoarsely as he waved the cane menacingly at Brother Mark. Brother Mark and Brother Jacob stopped, assessed the situation and backed off.

Eddy helped me up, and they took me to a sink to wash the blood from my face. My reflection fed my rage. I pushed Eddy and Uncle Alvin out of the way and went after Brother Mark. I was like a flailing disembodied spirit. My screams rang in my ears.

Uncle Alvin interceded again. I was in a blind rage, my mind in a numb state of shock. Brother Mark's anger matched my own.

"That's it. He is going to the cell." He now felt justified in doing what he wanted to do all along.

"No," said Uncle Alvin. "He is going to the infirmary with me." He told Eddy and my brothers to assist him in getting me there. This was probably to make sure that they were safe as well. Once he was out of the room, Brother Alvin probably felt that they would be used as scapegoats if he wasn't there to defend them.

I raged like a crazy person all the way to the infirmary. I screamed death threats and swore at Uncle Alvin for stopping me.

Once in the infirmary, all the fight had gone out of me, and I began to cry. My body had started to respond to the beating and the pain that had been inflicted upon it. Eventually I passed out from exhaustion as well as pain.

After I came to, the director came in, and sent Eddy and my brothers away. He told them that I would be all right. He shut the door behind them and then turned to Uncle Alvin.

"Robin is under house arrest as of now. Once you have finished cleaning him up, he will be taken directly to the cell."

Uncle Alvin convinced the director that I would not be able to go until the morning. I slept there with Uncle Alvin guarding over me during the night.

The next morning, Brother Jacob and the director came to take me to the cell. Uncle Alvin protested, "I will take him to the cell."

30

The four of us walked to the cell together since the director and Brother Jacob didn't trust Uncle Alvin to do it alone. Uncle Alvin didn't trust them to take me without me being on the receiving end of another punishment.

The cell was located in one corner of the second floor at the back of the building. A cement floor supported a seat-less toilet. A small sink with a cold water tap hung on the wall. The door was made of wood with two bars across the outside and an opening gridded with bars. A small cot pressed against one wall, and just above it was a barred window. I was ordered to strip and my clothes were replaced with a hospital gown. The gown was short and split up the back. I was not even permitted the dignity of underwear.

There was some haggling, and it finally was agreed that Uncle Alvin would bring me my meals. Uncle Alvin was so adamant about this that I don't think anyone wanted to argue with him.

Time dragged in that human cage. Depression cloaked my soul. Frustration and self pity displaced anger and hatred. I was alone with my thoughts and naked body. The hospital gown was in a heap on the floor. It seemed too cumbersome to wear and try to keep from falling forward. I spent my time exercising and keeping fit knowing that when I got out I would be involved in a lot more physical conflicts.

Three times a day, Uncle Alvin would come in with my meals and offer words of encouragement. When I heard the key in the lock, I would put on the hospital gown, out of respect for his sensitivity more than any modesty

I felt. I could feel his concern for me, but was so engulfed in my own despair, that I didn't even try to make him feel better. At that time, even Uncle Alvin was part of the focus of my anger. He knew of the unfair and unjust treatment, and he seemed unwilling to lift a finger to do anything.

Twice in three days, Brother Stephen came to see how I was doing. He brought my math workbook with some word problems to occupy my mind. I found it impossible to focus on them. For some reason, I didn't feel any anger toward Brother Stephen, even though he also was aware of the problems of abuse. Looking back, I don't know why that was. He was indeed younger, stronger and more likely to be heard than Uncle Alvin, but it didn't occur to me to think that he should do something.

On the second night, I stood on the cot which was under the window and looked through the bars into the night sky. I was focused on a particularly bright star and imagined myself there. After a while, I was staring blindly into the sky, and suddenly, I found that I was looking down on my naked form standing on the cot, looking out of the window. I was frightened and wondered if I was dead. I realized that my body would have been horizontal if that were the case, and my body was still standing.

I could not feel any part of that body, and I didn't know how I had got out or if I would be able to get back in. These thought raced through my mind, and the sensation lasted probably than a minute. I returned to my body as magically as I had left it. I felt a strange sense of awe as I lay down on the cot.

On the third day, I awoke to the sound of the bar being removed and the key turning in the lock. Uncle Alvin entered with my breakfast tray.

"How are you this morning, Robin?" He feigned cheerfulness, but he could not hide the lines of worry that had forged new routes in the road map of his face.

"Has anyone been to see you?" he asked.

"Only Brother Stephen and you," I replied.

"The director hasn't come?" He looked worried.

"No."

Uncle Alvin picked up a piece of my toast absentmindedly and took a bite. "Brother Gordon always comes after one day to get the boy's side of the story. I don't understand."

"Well," I said, taking a piece of toast before he ate it all. "He hasn't been here yet, and I've been home all the time." I made a feeble attempt at a smile.

He looked and me and stood up, noticing for the first time the half-eaten piece of toast in his hand. "I seem to have . . . I will get you more," he said.

"Never mind," I said. "I've had enough."

He put the partly eaten toast on the tray and went out again, coming back a while later with another two slices of toast.

Alone once more, I went through my exercise routine for about an hour. I stood and looked out of the window. There wasn't much to see. The window faced the building that housed the brothers' quarters. There was a narrow drive between the two buildings, and I could see the back end of the cemetery in the churchyard beyond the building.

There was a service truck in the drive, and a deliveryman was bringing some fresh bread. He must have sensed me looking at him because he looked up. His face showed shock when he glimpsed my battered face behind the bars. I waved at him, and he quickly jumped into his truck and drove away at a great pace.

I sat down and tried to focus on the math that Brother Stephen had brought me. My thoughts kept wandering back to the night before and my out-of-body experience. It no longer frightened me as I tried to figure out what had triggered it. I thought that maybe I could learn to control this experience and travel wherever I wanted. Then the bars on the cell could not hold me, and I would be able to remove myself from situations that I did not like or that were too painful.

That night, I was standing looking out at the moon and the stars, my hospital gown on the floor. I heard the cell door being unlocked with the key. I didn't turn around. I knew who it was without looking, or so I thought. I was expecting Brother Jacob. My body trembled in anticipation, and I told myself that I was strong and ready for him. I could feel the blood pounding in my head, and I turned to reach for my hospital gown—some sort of protection. I was shocked to see that there were two of them—Brother Jacob and Brother Mark. Now I had a real reason to be scared.

Each carried a strap, and both stared at me lecherously. They both removed their robes, and Jacob mimicked, "Till death do us part, eh?"

I jumped at him, and they both began to wield their straps. They hit me everywhere. I grabbed at their balls. Kicking and biting, I looked for their weak points. Of course, it didn't take them long to have me on the floor, and they applied the straps to the bottom of my feet.

Then the relief that I had prayed for had arrived. I was out of my body, and I was watching from the corner of the cell. My body was curled into a ball, and my arms covered my head while those two bastards beat the hell out of my body. I was unable to remove myself away from the sight of my body, and I was forced to watch. There was blood all over the place. My nose looked like pulp, and my arm was pointing in a strange direction. Brother Mark sneered over my body. His penis defying gravity and his hair electrified. His eyes were filled with hatred and lust, and he seemed to drool.

"Now give me the finger, you little fucker," he snarled as he kicked me in the face. "I'll show you my finger." Brother Jacob knelt down and turned my body onto its knees, forcing my head into his crotch. He grabbed the hair at the back of my head and pushed his penis into my mouth. Brother Mark crouched behind me and held my buttocks apart and shoved his erection into my rectum.

When Brother Mark finally shuddered to a finish, he pulled out and said, "It's been a long time since I have had a virgin."

Brother Jacob snickered and said, "You hold this end now." He stood up and went around the other end of my body. While Brother Mark held me down, Brother Jacob slammed into me with furious strokes and was shaking in the throes of his orgasm almost as soon as he entered. I could see blood from my anus added to the pool that was on the floor.

Then they were gone. I saw myself in a heap on the floor, and this time, I really thought I was dead.

I woke up on the floor on my side, feeling excruciating pain in my rectum. It overshadowed the screaming heat that was coming from my skin where I had been slashed with the straps. My arm was at a strange angle, my eyes were swollen shut, my nose seemed to be plugged with blood, and I had to breathe through my mouth. Every part of my body was yelling for attention. I didn't try to go through any more of the inventory and gratefully drifted back into unconsciousness. I heard the key in the lock, and Uncle Alvin gasped in shock as he dropped the breakfast tray on the floor. Light filtered through my eyelids, telling me that day had come, but I didn't feel inclined to unglue my eyes and face the horrors of consciousness. I fought to return to the blackness.

"Dear Lord," he whispered as he came to me and picked my head up and put it on his knee. "Brother Jacob? Brother Mark? Who?" he asked.

I nodded.

"Which one?" he asked.

"Both," I said.

"What have they done to you?" He knew the answer, and I didn't have the energy to tell him, let alone relive the devastation.

He sat me up and grabbed the bedsheet and wrapped it around me. I unglued my eyes and looked at the floor. It was covered in sticky, drying blood. It looked like a busy abattoir. I focused on Uncle Alvin as tears ran down either side of his anguished face. He held and rocked me as he knelt on the floor.

"I have to get help," he said, and seeing the fear in my eyes when I realized that he was going to leave me alone, he added, "I'll be right back. You will be okay."

"Please, please, call my mother!" I cried out to him. "I won't tell anyone if you just get my mother and tell her to come and get me."

Brother Alvin came right back and said he had sent Eddy to go and get Brother Stephen. He resumed holding me and muttering, "Animals, animals, you poor, poor boy."

Eddy arrived with Brother Stephen. He looked at me and began to weep. Eddy's face showed shock and horror. I didn't want him to see me like this. I didn't want him to look at me with pity. How could I ever look him in the face again? He would think of me as a faggot and a sissy. He would also think of me as a victim.

By now, the sheet that had covered me was drenched in blood. Brother Stephen stared and asked, "Who did this, Brother Alvin?" The muscle in his jaw was clenched.

"Who do you think?" asked Uncle Alvin. "Brother Jacob and Brother Mark." He spit out the names as if he had a mouthful of poison. "Here are my keys, open the door to the infirmary, and I will carry him."

Brother Stephen looked at the little old man and said, "I will carry him, Brother Alvin. You go and open the door."

"No! I will carry him!" roared Uncle Alvin.

To this day, I do not know how he did it. I outweighed him by twenty pounds, and it was at least fifty yards to the infirmary.

They put me in a tub and washed me in warm water. My skin was so raw that the water felt as if it was boiling. I was trembling uncontrollably, shaking until my bones and teeth rattled. I wept with a grief that owned my soul.

"Get my mother," I pleaded.

Anger took over, and I screamed, "Why isn't she here? Why is she not here looking after us? Why did she do this to us? I hate her!"

My anger toward her at that moment was even greater than the fury that I felt for Brothers Mark and Jacob. I didn't know where to start my vendetta of revenge. I was hysterical as Eddy and Uncle Alvin carried me over to the bed. Brother Stephen had gone and came back with the director.

"What in heaven's name!" He looked at me and then Uncle Alvin.

"They will pay for this," he vowed, not having to ask who was responsible; Brother Stephen had already told him.

"The police should be called," said Uncle Alvin to the director.

"No, no, Brother Alvin. We can't have that," said the director. "Think of what it would do to us, to the school. You do what you can for him, and we will decide what to do."

He turned and seemed to notice Eddy for the first time. He stared at him for a minute and said, "You go to your regular chores, and I'm warning you, not a word to anyone about this. Do you understand?"

Eddy was still crying. "I understand, I promise." He headed toward the door and then looked back at me. He tried to smile and gave me a little wave before going out the door.

The director turned to Uncle Alvin and Brother Stephen.

"Brother Stephen, you had better go down for breakfast and get ready for class. Brother Alvin, I will have someone bring up some breakfast for you and the boy."

Brother Stephen said that he would go to class and come back at noon so that Uncle Alvin could go and have lunch. Brother Alvin told him that he wasn't leaving me and that Brother Stephen could come and bring him lunch.

"I guess first," said Brother Stephen, "that we had better set that arm and see if he is in shock."

"Of course, he is in shock," said Uncle Alvin. I didn't know that anyone could look so old and tired.

I fell asleep, and when I woke, the sun was shining. My skin was on fire, and Uncle Alvin was asleep in the rocking chair next to my bed. My mouth was more swollen and dry than it had been the day before, and I found it difficult to speak. I felt like I had been through a thrashing machine, and I moaned.

Uncle Alvin jumped up, and I realized that this wonderful old man had not left me. He held a glass of orange juice with a straw to my lips. I could not suck the juice into the straw, and eventually, Uncle Alvin took a spoon and spooned the juice into my mouth. Swallowing was almost as painful as everything else, and I wondered what they had done to my throat.

I heard the director screaming at Brothers Jacob and Mark in the outer office. "If he doesn't pull through, you will both go to jail. You had better pray that he is all right. You must be crazy. Did you just leave him there to die? You are both very sick! Get out of here, and go back to you duties! If I hear of any more excuses, you will be out of here and reported to the Archdiocese."

Brother Gordon came to visit on an hourly basis and asked Uncle Alvin how I was doing.

"This boy should be in the hospital," was Uncle Alvin's response once.

"No, no," cajoled the director. "Go to the drug store, and get anything that you need for him. We want to keep this quiet."

The time in the infirmary was blurred. It lasted anywhere between ten days and two weeks. When I finally was allowed and able to get up, my body was weak, and I had to hang onto Uncle Alvin for support.

The bottoms of my feet still hurt from the strapping that they had received. While lying in bed, the desire for revenge was the only thing that I could think of, and I wanted to get up and get strong again. All the fear had left me. As far as I was concerned, I had suffered every form of abuse possible and nothing else could hurt me. My only thought was to kill those bastards.

31

Brother Stephen continued to instruct me in the finer points of fighting and boxing. I worked with him whenever we both had the time, and I practiced when he was unavailable. While Uncle Alvin was my sanctuary, Brother Stephen was my mentor and teacher, and I looked up to him as a kind of hero, father figure, big brother and friend.

One day, after a baseball game, I was putting the bats in the large duffel bag. I was alone on the field with the exception of Brother Mark. I was standing a few feet behind him as he bent down to do up his shoe. I saw an opportunity to use the bat on him and had extracted one from the bag when Brother Stephen came running out from nowhere, calling my name.

My opportunity was gone and part of me still regrets that I didn't kill the slimy low life. I guess my life would have changed a lot had I been able to follow my urge at that moment. Brother Mark seemed to realize what might have happened, and he looked at me strangely.

I ran up beside him, shaking in fury and said, "You will never lay another hand on me as long as you live. You are a fucking bastard, and if I get a chance, I will kill you."

Brother Stephen had reached me by then and took me by the shoulder, telling me to calm down.

"You don't know how angry I am that you stopped me. That slime deserves to die!" I was still screaming and panting in my fury. I was mad at the world.

Brother Stephen walked with me around the field until I had control of myself. I vowed that someday I would kill both Brother Jacob and Brother Mark.

That day was the first day since I left the infirmary that I had seen Brother Mark, and I had yet to run into Brother Jacob. He never seemed to be in the lunchroom when I had to go in there.

Something happened after that day in the field. I don't know if Brother Stephen went to the director and told him of the near incident and suggested that it would be better if I was discharged from the school or if Brother Mark did. I somehow doubt that Brother Mark would have brought himself to the attention of the director at this time, and I imagined that he too was keeping a low profile.

Very soon after that day, I was told that I would finish my term at a farm not too far from the village. I was given some clothes—not the ones I had arrived in, since I had grown a lot. I had a couple of pair of new jeans, a jacket, two shirts, socks, runners, underwear, a sweater, and a jacket. I don't know where they came from, but I assumed the school or the farmer, since I hadn't really heard from my mother for a month, and then I didn't really hear from here since I didn't open her letter.

32

Monsieur and Mme. Bordeau ran a small farm where they raised chickens for eggs. They had about 150 acres on which they grew corn and soy beans. It was a busy, noisy home with three boys, two dogs, and several barn cats. I was expected to help with the chickens, feeding and watering them, and mucking out the large building that housed them. I wasn't asked to do anything that their sons weren't expected to do, with exception of the youngest who was only two. I was being paid, and the money was banked for the time when I would leave here. I didn't have any use for the money since I didn't have anywhere to go and spend it.

I lived in the house with the family, and I was treated as one of them. The Bordeaus were a devout Catholic family, and we went to Mass every Sunday. M. Bordeau was a strong supporter of the school and, around four years prior to the time I was there, they had been approached by the school and asked if they were interested in helping the boys from the school to make the transition back to civilian life. They had willingly accepted, and I was the third boy who had moved in with them.

I had Saturday afternoons free and, after about two weeks at the farm, I had an urge to visit the school and see Brother Stephen, Uncle Alvin, Eddy, and my brothers. Even though the school had been the place of nightmares, it had been my home for a year and a half. At that time, I had grown from child to something in between life stages. The only attachments I had were still at the school, and I felt adrift with no land in sight.

Although the Bordeaus were kind people, they had no idea of what I had been through, and I felt rudderless without the school. I missed the people who knew me and the trials I had endured.

I walked into town and walked up the steps to the front door. I entered, and the director walked past without even noticing me. There were a few people in the hall, but no one spoke to me until I saw Uncle Alvin.

"What are you doing here, Robin?" He said this without his normal smile. "You don't belong here anymore."

"I came to see my brothers, Eddy, and Brother Stephen," I did not add Uncle Alvin's name since it seemed that he didn't want to see me. I didn't understand his lack of warmth at seeing me. I was hurt and confused. I didn't have a life, and this was the only substitute I had. I said in defiance, "I am going to first go and see Brother Stephen."

I went up the stairs to Brother Stephen's room and knocked on the door. He opened the door a crack and looked surprised to see me.

"Robin, what are you doing here?" His manner was nervous, and he pretended to smile. What the hell was going on here?

"I came to see you," I said with a smile.

"Okay, I am just getting dressed. I'll come right out." He pushed the door but it didn't latch.

I pushed the door open, and there was Brother Stephen putting on his robe. A boy of about five years was standing behind him next to the bed and wearing a frilly dress.

It took me a few seconds to realize what I was seeing. I turned and ran blindly out of the door.

"Robin! Robin, come back here," he yelled.

I kept running, wanting to jump out of the window at the top of the stairs. I somehow made my way out of the building and onto the street. Now my initiation to life was complete. Now the last vestige of humanity had revealed itself to me in the final blow of deceit.

I raced away without seeing or knowing where I was going. My feet moved faster than they had in any race they had been in. I tried to outrun my thoughts.

"Liar! Liar! Liar!" my brain screamed.

My heart pumped in rhythm to my screaming brain and pounding feet. The crashing, screaming, pounding orchestra continued its deafening racket. I could not outrun the pain. No matter how fast I went, the anguish kept easy pace. I had been robbed! I had been robbed of my belief in the assumption that a few shreds of human decency still existed.

I arrived at the bottom of a ravine on the river's edge. My heart was still pounding; there was pain in my sides, and I was gasping and choking with tears. My throat was closed by a piercing, white-hot pain. I was going to die of asphyxiation. I welcomed the thought. I waited for the merciful relief that death would bring.

I didn't die. Rage had replaced the pain and had taken possession of me. Its tenacity has a long lease on my soul. I embraced it. I hosted the rage and fed it, making sure that it did not ebb away from lack of nutrition.

33

I stayed at the river until dark. My face was streaked with dirt and tears when I finally found my way back to the Bordeau farm.

The house had originally been a small bungalow, and it had been added to as the family grew. There were sections covered with clapboard; some had stucco and others were sided with brick.

From the outside, it looked like a pattern for a crazy quilt. The kitchen was in the back of the house, and when I arrived, it was brightly lit as were most of the windows in the house. There was no way that I could sneak in and get to my bedroom which was off the kitchen. I couldn't stand the thought of facing anyone, so I went to the barn and climbed into the loft that was filled with bags of feed for the chickens, and straw for the floor of the chicken building. I was hungry and spent.

Fatigue made me forget about food, and it was no time before I fell asleep. I woke sometime later with a light shining in my eyes.

"Robin!" It was M. Bordeau. "We have been worried sick about you." He said this with sincere concern, and no evidence of anger.

I struggled upright and held my hand up to my eyes. He lowered the flashlight, and my eyes adjusted to my surroundings.

"Where have you been? When you didn't come in for supper we began searching. The kids scoured your usual haunts, and Marie is just frantic with worry. I called the school, and they said that you had been there and left in a hurry. Little Nikki cried himself to sleep. Where have you been since you left the school?" he probed.

"I went to the school," I said, even though he knew that.

He looked at me for a moment and asked, "Are you hungry?"

That was a dumb question; I was always hungry. The Bordeaus had always teased me about my appetite. I nodded, and he started to back down the ladder. "I'm sure we can find you something to eat. Come into the house, and Marie will get you something. She will be so relieved."

I followed him into the kitchen, and we found his wife, Marie, at the table darning socks. She looked up as we entered and exclaimed, "Oh, Robin! Look at you! Where have you been?" She put her arms around me and squeezed the air out of my lungs. "You are a mess! You must be hungry. Go wash your face and hands, and I will get you something to eat. How about some fried egg sandwiches?"

She made me smile as she fretted and asked nonstop questions, still hanging onto me.

M. Bordeau laughed and shook his head. "Marie, let the boy go. He can't breathe."

She reluctantly let go of me, wiping her hands on her apron. Then as I was about to go to the bathroom to wash up, she grabbed me again and gave me another big hug.

"Oh, I'm so glad you are back and safe," she exclaimed.

Finally, I was released, and I went to wash up as she began rattling around in the kitchen.

M. Bordeau was sitting at the kitchen table when I returned. His plump, hard-working wife was frying eggs. She then put ketchup and milk on the table. She went to the stove and turned on the kettle for tea, chattering all the while.

"We had pretty much given up on you," said M. Bordeau. "We had checked everywhere. I was just doing a yard check and noticed that the barn door was open. We had checked in there earlier, and I remembered closing the door, so I checked again. You had us very worried. Why didn't you come in the house?"

"My, yes!" said Marie. "I could barely get the kids to bed. They were so worried. Don't you ever again do that to us!" She tried to sound stern, but her relief overshadowed any other emotion that she tried to portray.

I sat across the table from M. Bordeau and looked around the big untidy kitchen and smiled. It was safe and warm. There was a clothesline strung across the side of the room and some of M. Bordeau's long johns hung near the stove along side of a bunch of parsley and another of sage.

Before she turned around, Marie pulled a handkerchief out of her apron pocket and wiped her eyes and blew her nose. She put the sandwiches on a plate and brought them to the table.

"Help yourself," she said.

I dove into the sandwiches as if I hadn't eaten in weeks, rather than fifteen hours. M. Bordeau picked up a sandwich, and Marie smiled contentedly. I munched my way through three sandwiches, and Marie drank a cup of tea while she watched me.

"Why don't you go to bed, dear," said M. Bordeau after she had finished her tea. "Robin and I will be along in a bit."

She looked from him to me and seemed to want to say something, but thought the better of it.

"Okay, but don't stay up too late," she said. She bent over her husband and kissed him on the top of the head, and then came around the table and did the same to me.

When she had gone, M. Bordeau said to me, "Now what's the story? You have been with us for a while now, and we don't know any more about you than we did when you first arrived from the school. We know that you are a good worker, and you have two brothers in the school. We know that because Brother Gordon gave us that fact when he called and asked if you could come and stay here. Did you go to the school to see your brothers?"

I lowered my head and looked through my eyelashes at him, and said, "Yes."

"What happened when you got there?" he asked. "Something must have happened since I heard you left in a hurry and didn't get back here for hours."

I didn't say anything. How could I tell him everything or anything? He was a strong supporter of the school. He wouldn't believe me. He and his family went to Mass every week, and they were strong believers in their faith. They said grace every meal and read the Bible every night after supper.

He waited, and the silence became unbearable. I had no grudge with this kind man, and I searched for something to say to him that would be plausible and justify my behavior.

"I missed my brothers, and I was worried about them, especially Peter. He isn't doing very well there, and he doesn't have any friends. I wanted to see if they were all right." I said this hoping it explained everything.

"Why didn't you tell us you were going? Something there upset you, and from what I hear, you didn't have time to see your brothers. Why did it take you so long to come back?"

I realized that I would have to elaborate a bit more. "I'm sorry for causing you so much trouble. I didn't even think that you would worry since I had done my chores." I don't know if I intended to sound martyred, but it came out that way, and I was immediately ashamed of myself for trying such a tactic with him.

"That isn't the point," he said with agitation. "Do you think that we have you in our home only until you disappear and then we can pretend that you don't exist? Do you not realize that we have made a commitment to you and the school? Can you not see that our reaction is one of concern for you? We have taken you into our home, but we have also found space for you in our hearts. What kind of Christians would we be if we just let you wander off and not worry about you?"

This was the biggest problem, in my eyes. His faith prevented me from telling him any part of the sordid story. I couldn't give him credit for being able to separate the church and its institutions from his religious beliefs. I didn't have the language or the insight to explain in any way that didn't work counter to his faith. If he believed me, I thought that he would have to denounce his faith. If he didn't believe me, he would have to denounce me, leaving me alienated once again.

I sniffed as tears of frustration filled my eyes. He looked across at me and softened.

"I have watched you since you came here. You have the eyes of an old man. You look old and disillusioned at far too young an age. You need to find Christ."

I physically balked and said nothing.

"I need to know you. Is it that you miss your brothers? Are you homesick," he asked.

I grasped at this to escape the dilemma of explanation. I nodded and kept my head down.

"You know, Robin, there is nothing tying you here. I can make arrangements for you to go home. You have some money coming that has been banked for you by the school while you work here. Do you want to go home?" He said this in a defeated tone.

I thought about this. I had forgotten home, and wondered what the reception would be. Did my mother want me? What would I do? Where else could I go?

"I want to talk to my brothers before I go, but yes, I think I would like to go home," I said.

"Okay, tomorrow, I will call the school and arrange for you to visit your brothers," said M. Bordeau with decision.

The thought of going back to the school was terrifying. "Please, not the school!" The words came up from my heart instead of their usual route through my brain.

For a long minute, he looked at me before saying, "Maybe we could take them out for a Coke or something. I think the school knows me well enough to let them come out and see you for a short visit."

I hoped he was right and said, "Could I wait for them somewhere else while you pick them up?"

Again, he looked at me, trying to figure out what I was leaving unsaid. "What happened today, or rather, yesterday at the school?" he asked again.

"Nothing. They just didn't want me there." I tried to make it sound as simple as that.

"I know there is something that you are not telling me, and if it is that you did something wrong when you were there, they will tell me when I call."

He waited for me to confirm or deny this, and when I said nothing, he continued, "Now then, it is time for bed."

It was 2:30 a.m.

"Six o'clock comes early, and the eggs will have to be packed tomorrow for the truck coming Monday morning."

He picked up the dishes from the table and put them in the sink. I got up and headed for my little room that had once been the pantry off the kitchen.

My room. It was small and safe and private. What a luxury. I fell asleep somewhere between being vertical and being horizontal.

34

"Robin! Robin!" Hands were shaking my shoulders, and Andrew and James were grinning at me. I groaned as they sat on the edge of my bed.

"Where did you go? We thought you were dead!" said James.

"It kind of feels like that right now," I responded. "Am, I? What time is it?"

"Six. Get up," said Andrew.

Oh well, four-and-a-half-hours sleep was better than no sleep. I felt like I had been dragged through a hedge backward. I stumbled to my feet, pulled on yesterday's jeans and headed for the bathroom. Andrew and James followed me with a tirade of questions. I didn't have time to answer one question when the next was fired at me. This was just as well since I couldn't think well enough to come up with acceptable answers.

"Why isn't Papa mad at you," asked James.

"I don't know." This question I could answer honestly.

We finally went into the kitchen to find Marie fussing over the stove, and little Nikki was sitting in his highchair banging a spoon on the tray.

Marie told us that M. Bordeau was already in the chicken barn. He came in as we sat at the long narrow table. "I've fed the chickens and changed the straw on the floor and the cages. We'll have to collect the eggs and pack them in the cold cellar. Then we have to clean up and change for church. I will call the school before we leave for church and set up a meeting with your brothers later this afternoon."

How did he do it? I looked at him and realized that he must have had less than two hours sleep. He smiled at me and looked around at his family in quiet pleasure. Marie brought a platter of scrambled eggs and another of sausages to the table. She put some eggs in a bowl for Nikki and returned to the oven for the toast being kept warm inside. From the coffee pot on the stove, she filled a cup for herself and one for her husband. Finally, she sat down, and we bowed our heads as M. Bordeau said grace.

"May the Lord be thanked for our home and family and the safe return of Robin, and may we be truly thankful for the food we are about to receive. Amen."

He looked up and said, "Dig in everyone."

Andrew and James both began talking at once. They told me they were glad I was back. Nikki, whose chair was next to mine, hit me on the shoulder with his spoon and yelled, "Robin!"

He reminded me of little Mary at Crystal and John's house. I hadn't thought of them in a long time and for the first time in months, I knew what I felt homesick for; a real home that I was a part of. I realized that I would feel homesick for this place when I left as well. The two places I felt a sense of home were homes that I hadn't been born into. I got a lump in my throat and forced myself to focus on the conversation around the table.

"How much will we get for the eggs tomorrow, Papa?" asked Andrew. "Do you think that we will have enough left over to buy Jimmy's bike down the road?"

"I don't know, son," said his father. "Have you saved any money from your allowance?"

"I have four dollars and thirty-seven cents," Andrew proudly announced.

"Well, that is almost half of the price of the bike, and that is what we agreed on. If you promise to give me the other sixty-three cents from next week's allowance, I will give you the difference when I get the egg money, if that's all right with your Mama." He looked at Marie and smiled.

"I guess that is all right if you don't mind eating porridge for a week," teased Marie.

"No way," protested James. "Andrew can eat porridge for a week; it's his bike."

Everyone laughed, including Andrew.

While Marie cleaned up and Nikki threw his toast on the floor, the rest of us went out to the barn to finish up the chores. We didn't have too much to do, since M. Bordeau had done most of the chores. We gathered the eggs and stored them, then went into the house to get cleaned up for church.

Marie was at the kitchen sink washing some tea towels. The wringer washer had been pushed up to the sink, and she was doing some of the endless washing. "Your other jeans are clean, Robin, and when you take the ones you are wearing off, bring them out here so that I can wash them later. They are filthy."

I looked over at the clothesline and saw my second pair of jeans hanging closest to the stove.

With exception of Sunday, Marie worked nonstop all day, every day, except for church and the occasional visit with neighbors. In the evening, she would sit and mend or knit while they listened to the radio, or while her husband read the Bible. On Sundays, we would get into the station wagon and go to church in Parques. After church, we would come home, and she would manage to prepare a hot lunch and wait for visitors.

The weather had been nice the last two Sundays, and we had sat on the porch drinking iced tea. Neighbors would drive up the long driveway, and come and sit a while. The men would talk about the weather and the price of crops, eggs, beef, etc. The women would talk about their children, recipes, crafts, the people who had shown up for church, and those who had not. Usually, the visitors had kids, and they would play with the Bordeau kids. Sunday was the one day I felt left out. Most of the kids were too young, even the ones my age. I wanted to go off by myself at these times, but, although it was never said, I felt it was expected of me to be there. I felt like an outsider, even though everyone made a great effort to make me a part of the group. I would hover between the adults and the kids, and sometimes play with Nikki. Sundays made me feel lonely.

That morning when we came into the house M. Bordeau said, "I will call the school now and see what we can arrange." He went to the phone, and my ears strained as I sat in the kitchen. Although I could hear him talking, I couldn't make out what was being said. Marie chattered away, and Nikki crawled up on my lap. He reached for my lemonade and knocked it over.

"Nikki," Marie scolded, "Get down now!" She came over and picked him off my lap. Nikki squawked while she scolded me for spoiling him.

"Maybe Robin would like some coffee instead," said M. Bordeau as he came into the kitchen.

"Jack!" she admonished.

"I think he is old enough to have some coffee if he would like some," said M. Bordeau. "He probably could use it since he didn't get too much sleep. We don't want him snoring in the church, do we?"

The thought of having coffee pleased me. I had tasted it, but had never been offered it.

Marie reluctantly brought a cup out of the cupboard and half filled it with coffee, topping it up with milk. She offered the sugar bowl, and I was allowed to doctor it myself. I sipped it unsweetened first then added three spoonfuls of sugar. I felt that the offer of coffee from M. Bordeau was a statement of some kind.

I waited for him to speak, and he finally said, "I can meet your brothers at the school at four o'clock. They must return by five-thirty."

We went to the church shortly after, and I spent the time wondering what I would say to my brothers about going home, when they would still be in the school. It would not seem fair to them, since we were all sent there for the same crime. I didn't know what I would say, and I knew that I couldn't make any promises about getting them out since we had all given up on promises. I didn't even know if my mother would take *me* back home.

After church and lunch at home, the usual visitors arrived. M. Bordeau excused himself from his visitors around 3:00 and said that he and I had to go out for a while. He encouraged them to stay as long as they liked.

We left the house and drove into town in his old pick-up truck. I was deposited at the café after M. Bordeau had gone in with me and told the waitress that I was to wait there for him, and that he would be right back. The café was just around the corner from the school. It wasn't very many minutes before he returned with Peter and Paul. M. Bordeau sat next to me in the booth, and Peter and Paul sat across from us. There was an awkward silence which M. Bordeau broke by saying, "What will it be boys? How about a cherry Coke?"

"Sure," we said in unison. We had never tasted it, but it sounded like it might be all right.

We got our drinks, and M. Bordeau drank his coffee.

Nobody said anything for a minute, and M. Bordeau said, "Look, I'm going over the counter to talk to Fred and Joe. You guys don't need me."

He got up and walked over to the counter with his coffee. He sat with the two men already there. The only other customer in the place was well out of hearing range.

"How are you guys doing?" I asked when we were finally alone.

"Just fine for prisoners," answered Paul with a sad smile.

Peter said nothing.

"What happened yesterday," Paul asked. "Some of the guys saw you running from the school like a scared rabbit."

"I tried to see you guys, and they wouldn't let me," I over-simplified. "Listen, I need to talk to Eddy. Can you talk to him?" I directed this to Paul. Peter didn't even seem to be there. He just slurped his Coke.

"Yeah, I see him at supper. How are you going to manage that though," asked Paul.

"Ask him if he can be outside the kitchen around one o'clock tomorrow. M. Bordeau comes into town to get his egg money and buy supplies and feed for the chickens. I usually come with him for the ride. I'll go to the alcove by the kitchen door, where the delivery trucks come. Eddy should be doing the clean-up chores around then. I can wait until quarter to two, and then I will have to go," I said.

"Okay, I'll tell him. How is the farm," Paul wanted to know.

"It's okay," I said, "The people are really nice, but I'm going home."

"Home?" This was the first word Peter had spoken since he got there.

"Yeah. I don't know how Mama will take it since I haven't heard from her in a long time," I said.

"She got tired of writing you when you didn't answer her letters. She doesn't know that you never opened them. She still thinks that she can get us out, but she doesn't write as much. She's seeing a new guy, and I think he is living there. Alexi moved back to Welford and is staying with Jacquelyn. He is apprenticing to become a mechanic at old Mr. Maudsley's garage."

Nothing stayed the same. I hadn't considered Mama having a new beau and him living with her. I put it to the back of my mind and decided to face that when I got there.

"I guess it's time to go, boys," said M. Bordeau as he approached the table. He looked at me and asked, "Do you want to wait here until I return, Robin?"

"Yes, please," I said, not looking at him.

When he returned, I was in front of the café. The waitress seemed to be tired of me, and I think that she wanted to close.

"Did you have a nice visit," asked M. Bordeau as I got into the car.

"Yeah, sure," I said. "Err, can I come to town with you tomorrow?"

"If you like," he said. "I guess we won't have you too much longer. I'll phone your mother tonight." He seemed to be forcing himself to be positive. "We are all going to miss you, but we are happy for you."

I didn't know what was going to greet me at home, and I hoped that there would a reason to be happy about going home.

"Your brothers seem like nice boys." He went on, "Peter—is that the older one? He seems troubled."

"That's an understatement," I said to myself. Out loud, I said, "He's just shy."

We drove in silence for a while, and then M. Bordeau cleared his throat and asked, "Is there something wrong at that school?"

How I wanted to tell him!

"They are just strict, that's all," I said instead.

"Well, there is nothing wrong with a little discipline." He leaned over and turned up the radio to listen to the farm report. "I have to fix that spot in the eaves trough when we get home. Do you think you can feed the chickens?"

"Sure," I said.

When we got out of the car, I went directly to the barn and walked around, feeding the chickens. I think chickens are smellier than pigs or cows. I was just about used to the stench, but I thought that it was the one thing that I wouldn't miss. I was hoping that Paul had managed to talk to Eddy and that I would see him the next day.

I thought about the phone call that M. Bordeau was going to make to my mother that evening with some trepidation. What if she didn't want me? Would I be able to hide my anger with her when I went home? I had no desire to be on her wrong side since I had to live somewhere. I had always been able to hide my feelings from her in the past, but I had never been put through such turmoil when I had lived with her. I didn't really want her to know how angry I was with her. Right now, I was riding an emotional roller coaster, and hiding my emotions might be difficult.

I heard Andrew calling me in for supper. I reluctantly went into the house, leaving my thoughts behind. When the kids were home, I seldom had time for my own thoughts. They still treated me like a new toy. Not that I minded most of the time; it was kind of flattering.

I entered the kitchen, and Andrew and James shouted their greetings from just five feet away.

"Hey, guys." I smiled. "How's it going?"

"Great," said Andrew. "As soon as we are finished supper, I can go down to Jimmy's and get the bike! Dad said that he didn't have to wait for the egg money, and I can have it today."

He was all smiles, and I was happy for him. I looked at James to see what his response was. James was nine, and I expected him to show some signs of envy.

"James," said Andrew, "maybe I could show you how to ride."

"Maybe," mumbled James.

Andrew turned to me and said, "James tried to ride the bike at the Thomas's house one day, and he fell off in front of a car. He's still nervous about that."

"So am I," said his mother. "I'm nervous about you too, Andrew. I hope you ride safely and on the right side of the road."

"Now, Marie," said M. Bordeau, "you have to let them grow up."

"I don't see why," she responded. "Being grown-up is not all that it's cracked up to be."

We let the subject drop and talked of other things. As soon as we finished supper, Andrew jumped up and ran to the door, calling back, "I'll be right back with my new bike!"

"James," said Marie. "Why don't you put Nikki in the bathtub, and I'll clean up the dishes." She then looked at me and said, "Maybe, Robin, you could dry the dishes for me."

"Sure," I said, a little surprised. She had never asked me for help in the kitchen before, and I had never thought of offering. I got up and helped her clear the table, and Nikki followed James to the bathroom.

"I'll go and make that phone call now," said M. Bordeau as he pushed himself away from the table."

I felt nervous and wondered what would happen. My feelings were mixed about him making the call. I didn't want to hear unless the news was good, and I would never have had the nerve to ask my mother on my own for fear of rejection and embarrassment. I hoped that M. Bordeau would soften the blow if my mother said I couldn't go home.

I dropped a glass, and it shattered on the floor.

"I'm sorry," I said as I bent down to pick up the pieces off the floor.

"Don't use your hands to pick up broken glass, honey," said Mary. "Let me get the broom, and you hold the dustpan." She went to the corner where the broom and dustpan stood in readiness for service at all times.

Once the glass was swept away, we resumed the task of cleaning up the supper dishes. Marie chatted away at her nonstop pace. I only half listened to her, trying to hear what was being said on the phone and not really wanting to know until it had been safely edited, as I knew M. Bordeau would do if there was something that would hurt my feelings.

Eventually, M. Bordeau came into the kitchen and looked troubled. I held my breath and waited. Marie turned to look at her husband and stopped talking.

"Tell me, Robin, what happened at the school," he asked me.

"What do you mean?" I really didn't know what he was talking about. So many things had happened at the school.

"Well, your mother thought you were still there, and you have been here for over a fortnight. Nobody told her. You didn't write? They didn't write?"

"Err, no. I thought the school would do it. I was going to, but I just haven't gotten around to it," I stuttered.

I could hear James yelling at Nikki, telling him to keep the water in the tub. For once, Marie was without words, and the Bible session was forgotten.

"I'm going to take your helper, Marie," said M. Bordeau. "It is time that young Robin and I had a talk."

To me, he said, "Let's go outside and see if the soybeans have sprouted."

I followed him in fear. What would I do if I had no place to live? I was only thirteen, and I felt that M. Bordeau and Marie wanted me to leave. I lagged behind, trying to put off the bad news.

A dented, silver cigarette case was pulled out of M. Bordeau's shirt pocket. The silver had mostly worn off. He opened it and removed a hand-rolled cigarette, sticking it into his mouth. He then reached into his pants' pocket and extracted an equally worn silver Zippo and lit the cigarette. He took a long drag and slowly exhaled.

"I'm not going to force you to tell me anything you don't want to," he said. "Let's sit on the bench behind the barn where we can see the sunset."

I followed him behind the barn, and we sat on the bench in silence for a moment. I forced myself to look straight into his face, fearing what I might encounter.

He stared right back at me and smiled with his honest, open face. "Robin, I talked to your mother first and learned that she didn't know that you had left the school. That, I already told you. I asked her if she would send your train and bus fare. I know that you have enough money in the bank to pay for it, but I thought that, if she could afford to pay, it would leave you with something when you got home. She thinks that you blame her for sending you to the school, and she is as afraid, as you are, of your next meeting. She told me of the events that led up to you being brought to the school in Parques, and all her efforts to get you back. She really loves you, and it is unfortunate that her efforts to change the situation have been in vain. She said that she would wire the money for your fare, and you could come home as soon as it can be arranged."

I hadn't known that I was holding my breath, but I let out a sigh. At least she still knew who I was and thought about us once in a while.

"She also said," continued M. Bordeau, "That, before you came to Parques, you stayed at the Barney's house outside of Fort St. Luke. I know John Barney. He and I belong to the Catholic Youth Council and have gone to conferences in Montreal together. I phoned him, and we talked briefly about you. He thinks highly of you and, although he seems to have been able to get through to you more easily than I; he and are of like mind when it comes to children, and the Church. We are not as blind as you might think about the flaws in the Catholic Church. One thing he told me about you was that you were loyal and sensitive. I can only do something about the things I am aware, and I don't go looking for trouble under every rock. I strongly suspect that you have, in some way, been abused or been mistreated, and that you feel that the whole world is out to get you. I will listen with an open mind and, anything you do not want broadcast, will be between you and me. I won't even talk to Marie about it."

A ray of hope was forming in my mind as I listened to him. He wasn't as easy to talk to as John was. I addressed him as M. Bordeau, and thought of him as my boss. He was a decade older and of a more serious bent than John. I realized from the first that he was a good man, and maybe that was the biggest barrier. I no longer thought of myself as a good person. All the time I was at the school, my thoughts had been polluted with dreams of revenge and hatred. I would never have the calm serenity that both John Barney and Jack Bordeau seemed to have. I looked at the world through muddy waters and hid my thought from all but Eddy. I felt evil by the association with evil, and my dirty soul was already in hell.

We sat in silence for a bit. I wanted to say something, but didn't know how to start.

He seemed to sense this and asked, "Did you get beaten at the school?"

I couldn't suppress my sneering laugh. "Yeah," I said looking down at my feet.

"Do you want to talk about it?" he prodded.

"I don't know. It would take so long to tell you. You wouldn't believe me anyway." I said this in an accusing tone, trying to put him on the side of all the bad guys I knew.

"Why don't you try me? Did I tell you that I was raised in foster homes until I finally ran away at thirteen?" He said this simply as a matter of fact, with no inflection in his voice.

I looked again at him, finding it hard to believe that this calm, well-adjusted man had endured anything but the kind of childhood that he was providing his children. He smiled down at me, pulling out another cigarette and lit it, giving me time to absorb this information.

"Why don't you start at the beginning, when you first were caught in the arena. Yes, I know about that. I had to know what kind of person I would have living here under my roof with my children. If you had murdered someone, or been violent, I wouldn't have been able to bring you here."

I took a big breath and asked him what he wanted to know.

"Well, you don't need to tell me why you went into the arena and did the things you did, I can understand that. Kids will always do things like that. I don't expect you to explain why you were given such extreme punishment as being taken from your home for such a minor crime. I'm sure that you don't know any more than I do. Why do you blame your mother?"

"It was because my mother was bootlegging," I said. "They decided that she wasn't fit to look after us. They said we would become criminals if we continued to live in the same house as her. I have two older sisters and two older brothers who haven't become criminals by living with her, but they decided that the three of us would."

I let it hang there, not wanting to tell him that the court had said that my mother was running a house of ill repute. During my stay at the school, I had often thought about that. When I was angriest with her, I would convince myself that it was true, in order to keep stoking the rage that burned inside me against her. I didn't want to admit to him that there was any other cause for the council to put us in the school. I wanted to appear the innocent victim of an unjust society.

"Was your mother raising you on your own," he asked.

"Yes," I said. "My father left us when Paul was just a few months old."

"Did she have any other job," he queried.

"We moved to Auburn after the restaurant she worked in was sold. She got a job cooking at the logging camp and then the camp closed down. She made pies and cakes and worked in a small café in town and at the tavern. She made out okay, but then somehow people started coming to our house when the tavern closed, and Mama would sell drinks at our house. She had a lot more money then, and she didn't have to work outside the house. There were lots of other people doing the same, but Mama was the one they decided to punish. Mama—and us."

We looked across the field and green fuzz had just started sprouting from the brown soil. The sun was low in the sky. We could hear Andrew calling us to come and see his bike. I could see M. Bordeau being pulled between his son and me.

He cleared his throat and said, "Wait right here. If I don't go and see the bike, there will be no end of him pestering me to do so." He smiled and hurried off.

While he was gone, I thought about my mother, and my words had made me realize that she wasn't guilty of anything but trying to raise her family in the best way she knew. I finally forgave her. I forgave her for not having the power to change things, and I forgave her for her faith in the Church. All the time I was at the school, I thought she knew every detail of each abuse. I realized that she was in the dark about all of it. I couldn't hold her responsible for her ignorance—an ignorance that I contributed to by not even communicating in the limited way that we had.

"I hope that the break in our conversation hasn't shut you up, now that you have begun to talk," said M. Bordeau when he returned to the bench. "What is it? You look relieved."

I struggled to find the words of gratitude I felt toward him. "Err, I guess when I told you about my mother, I realized that she didn't do anything wrong. Well, maybe in the opinion of the law, but not in the law of motherhood. I guess I have blamed her because if she was still a cook at the camp, we would have only been fined or something. She couldn't help the fact that the camp closed. There wasn't any work around, most of the businesses closed and lots of people moved away. She was happier there than she was in Welford. She had friends, and didn't have to 'rob Peter to pay Paul,'" I said with a smile as I remembered Mama's joke.

"When I talked to your mother, I knew that she loved you. She cried when she heard you were coming home and asked about your brothers. I told her that I had met them this afternoon, and she asked about them. I told her that Peter was quiet and shy. She didn't believe it. She said that Peter was never shy. She said that he was never good at taking responsibility for his own acts, but that he wasn't shy." He left it there, inviting me to respond.

I thought about Peter and forced myself to look at the reason he had become so quiet. I wondered about how much I could tell this man, but already the relief of the little I had shared had helped so much.

"It's a very long story, and it will take more than all night to tell you," I said.

"I guess I can do without sleep again, I can always go back to bed after the truck leaves. That is if Nikki will let me." He said this with a smile. "I would rather hear the story and let you shirk your chores in the morning. How did you like the Barneys? Is Crystal as lovely as John says?"

The thought of Crystal made me smile. "Oh, she is beautiful!" I couldn't help myself. Her face appeared before me, and I could hear her laugh that matched her name, clear and sparkling like crystal.

"I can see that you are almost as smitten with her as John," said M. Bordeau.

I blushed and stuttered, "She is like a magic fairy. She seems to travel on a beam of sunshine." I couldn't explain. "John is very lucky. When he comes into the room, her face lights up, and he is so happy. I think that they couldn't live without each other and be all that they are together. I don't think that that happens very often with people. That isn't the way it was for Mama and Papa." I didn't really want to think about my father.

Another cigarette was lit by M. Bordeau, and I thought about the Barneys. That week had been a very happy one for me and my brothers, even if it marked the end of all innocence.

Without prompting, I began to talk again. "When John took us to the train station, I really felt that I was leaving home. Their home was so carefree and happy. Not that our house was unhappy, but Mama was always working to make enough money to feed us; she never had any time for play. Crystal seemed to make the whole day seem like one giant game. You couldn't be unhappy when she smiled or laughed."

As the sun collided with the horizon, M. Bordeau prompted me to continue the story. I told him of the train ride, and all the trouble we caused for poor Arthur. He laughed out loud as I related our adventures. I halted my story when we got to the school.

"You are a bit of a devil, Robin." He said this with some admiration in his voice.

I smiled and shrugged my shoulders. "I guess I was."

The kind of devil he was talking about was not the devil I had become since. The first one had been impish and fun, without hatred or malice. The latter one was not fun and had a lot of venom and bile.

One of the dogs had found us and jumped up on me. I was glad of the distraction, not knowing if I wanted to venture into the next chapter of my life—*the school chapter*. M. Bordeau seemed to sense this and reached over and smoothed the dog's head, scratching him behind his ears. We sat in easy silence for a while, watching the stars appear in the clear sky. The moon had waned to a sliver, and the crickets were making a racket in the weeds that grew behind the barn, and in the firewood. I felt more peaceful than I had in a long time. I realized that I had managed to step away from the school, but knew that recounting the events that followed our entering those doors would be reliving them. I wanted to put it off, but somehow I realized that I had to purge those memories in order to heal and be whole again.

"When you got to the school, did Brother Alvin shake your hands and say you were good boys," asked M. Bordeau, interrupting my thought.

I laughed, "Oh sure. He told us that a lot, but I got the feeling yesterday, that he wished he had never met me. I bet he will quit his job and become a garbage man!"

For some reason, the thought tickled me. M. Bordeau joined in my amusement. "Anything that he could wish on us, though, couldn't be as bad as what really happened."

I waited for a prompt from him, knowing that I couldn't just spill it out without his help, and M. Bordeau obliged me, knowing just how to make it easier. He wasn't that different from John after all.

I began at the first night and started the telling. I didn't get all the facts in chronological order and would have to go back and explain things. He asked very few questions and just let me talk. I couldn't see his face, but I could feel the change in his presence. There was a tension in the air, and I became afraid to stop talking. I feared his pity or even worse. I was afraid that now I had opened up to him, he wouldn't believe me.

The stars started to fade as the night left the sky. The rooster crowed, and I finished telling M. Bordeau the entire story, with the exception of the encounter with Brother Stephen the day that I had returned to the school. Somehow I couldn't face that, even in my mind. Of all the pain that I had had inflicted upon me, and all that I had seen, that was the worst of all. I felt deceived and betrayed. Maybe that was because it was the newest, and I had yet to learn how to live with it.

I stopped talking, and he said nothing. He was very still and for a second, I thought he must have gone to sleep. I sat and waited for some reaction. He slowly turned to me with anger etched deep around his eyes.

He still said nothing. He nodded and stood up. I was confused. If he disbelieved me, I wished he would call me a liar to my face. One thing that did happen, even if I wasn't believed, was that I had managed to put the situation at a more comfortable distance from myself.

I didn't know if I should stand with him or remain on the bench. Finally, he looked at his watch and said, "Its five-thirty, I think that those chickens could be fed now and their eggs collected. If I talk real nice to Marie, she might look after the truck that picks up the eggs, then we could both go to bed and sleep uninterrupted for a few hours."

I followed him into the barn, totally exhausted. We went through the motions and managed to finish up our chores just as the kitchen light came on. Marie was at the kitchen sink starting to prepare for breakfast. He turned and put his hand on my shoulder and sighed, "Sacra Bleu. I don't know what to say to you. I will tell you one thing—I will not ignore the situation. This changes my plans though."

I didn't know what his plans were, and I didn't feel that I could ask. I did think that my voice had been heard, and it gave me hope.

Marie looked at us and said, "Where have you two been all night?"

"Would you believe we have been feeding the chickens?" M. Bordeau walked over to her and gave her a big hug.

"Not all night, I wouldn't." She smiled at him and then looked over at me. "You must be very tired. I know you are hungry; you are always hungry."

I didn't know if I could stay awake to eat anything, but I sat at the table and Marie got two coffee mugs out of the cupboard and filled on with coffee and half filled the other with coffee, topping it up with milk. I was beginning to like the idea of having such an adult drink. I hadn't noticed the cold when we were outside, but the warmth of the kitchen seemed to bring my body some comfort. I wrapped my hands around the coffee mug for warmth.

"Robin and I will need to get some sleep. Do you think that you could be here when the egg truck comes and get them to load up themselves? You just need to be there to make sure that we get credit for all the eggs. They don't always know how to count," M. Bordeau said to Marie.

The boys began to make themselves heard, Nikki was yelling to be let out of his crib, and Andrew was telling him to be patient. James was the first one in the kitchen.

"Robin, how come you are up so early?" Didn't you go to bed?" He smiled at his joke.

"Something like that," I said and smiled back.

"James, you can start making some toast. Your silly father and Robin have been out behind the barn all night. If we don't feed them real soon, they will be asleep at the table," said his mother.

"What were they doing?" He turned and looked at our tired faces, "Why did you do that?"

"We were just making plans," replied his father.

"What plans?" James wasn't giving up with vague answers.

"Don't be so nosy, son," intercepted Marie.

"Well, gee. I don't know what the big secret is anyway," complained James.

"If we told you, it wouldn't be a secret then, would it?" His father ruffled his hair and gave him a hug. "We were just having a private discussion, that's all."

James seemed to be satisfied, but when Andy came in the kitchen, James said, "Guess what? Robin and Dad sat behind the barn all night."

Andrew looked from his father to me and asked, "Is that fox back again, trying to get the chickens?"

"No. Remember, I shot him in the winter. There is nothing wrong. Robin and I just needed to have a long talk, but right now, I think we are all talked out." M. Bordeau had had enough of the questions, and I was glad that he had fielded them for me.

Nikki was demanding breakfast, and I let the commotion swirl around me. The next thing I knew, Marie was helping me into my room and taking my shoes and socks off for me.

"I guess you won't starve if you wait and eat after you have had some sleep," she said.

I lay down and gratefully pulled the covers up to my ears. "I guess I am a little tired," I said.

35

I dreamed that M. Bordeau thought I was lying, and he reported me to the director at the school. I was forced to go back to the school and wear a dress and red lipstick. I was in a room with chickens and faceless men in long black robes. They formed a circle around me while they bit off the heads of the chickens and threw them at me.

I woke with a start. My sheets wee soaked, and my hair was matted to my head. I got up slowly and went to the door of the kitchen. There was total silence. I wandered through the house and found no one there. I glanced at the clock and saw that it was two thirty. Eddy! They must have gone to town without me. Or maybe they had gone to the school, as I had dreamed, to report me to the director. I panicked. I was ready to run. The thought of returning to the school as a resident terrified me.

My stomach was sending urgent messages for food. My stomach's demands had seniority over my fears, and I went to the fridge. I made a bologna sandwich and poured myself a glass of milk. I heard the truck coming and went to the front room to see that the Bordeaus had returned. The truck pulled around the back, and I heard Marie scolding Nikki as the doors banged. Their faces gave no indication of betrayal as they unloaded the truck.

Marie came in and said, "Well, it looks like sleeping beauty is awake."

I looked at M. Bordeau when he finally came in and realized that these people hadn't betrayed me. He smiled at me and said, "I didn't want to wake you. I know you said you wanted to go into town, but you said that before you stayed up all night after only having a couple of hours sleep the night before. If you want, you can come in with me tomorrow, I have to go back and pick up some things."

Maybe they had betrayed me, and he was planning on taking me back tomorrow! I was muddled and confused.

"Er, no. I guess I don't need to go," I said.

He looked at me and must have seen the confusion on my face and asked, "What's wrong, Robin?"

"Nothing," I muttered.

"So we are back to that are we? You may be able to keep a lot of things inside, but you wear your feelings on your face." He came closer and said, "I'm sorry for not waking you. I didn't realize that it was important."

"It's okay. I just had a real weird dream. I dreamed you had made me go back to the school."

He looked shocked. "I didn't imagine that you thought me a cruel man, Robin. Well, maybe that is unfair for me to think that you could think of me any other way when I think about it. Cruelty is what you have become accustomed to."

He put his arm around my shoulder and said, "I guess it is up to me to prove that not all men are cruel and sadistic."

Marie watched this exchange wordlessly while she put away the groceries. The bafflement on her face told me that he had not told her the things that we had talked about.

The phone rang and Marie scurried out of the kitchen to answer it. She was back in a minute and told her husband that it was for him. She said to me, "Did you get something to eat, you must be starving. You couldn't stay awake for breakfast. How would you like an egg sandwich?"

"Sure," I said. "I did have a sandwich, but I can always eat another."

She laughed and went about doing the things she did best—looking after everyone. When M. Bordeau came back into the kitchen, she took a look at his face and exclaimed, "Jack, what is it?"

I looked at his ashen face and knew that he must have had a terrible shock. I felt cold and knew that somehow the news affected me. He sat at the table and buried his head in his hands and began to cry. Fear gripped my heart, and Marie went to him and kept asking him what was wrong.

I didn't want to know. Please don't let me hear, I prayed. Please say that nothing is wrong. Don't tell me that someone is dead. Let it be someone I don't know. Please. Please. No more grief! I had stood up and was ready to run.

He looked up with pity in his eyes. "Sit down, Robin. Turn off the stove Mary, you're burning the eggs. Nikki, go and find your toys."

Nikki protested and his father asked, "Do you want to go down for a nap, young man?"

"No!" he wailed.

"Then go to your room and play with your toys for a little while." He turned Nikki toward the door, and Nikki reluctantly headed to his room.

I sat, even though I wanted to bolt. I tried to turn my ears off. I squeezed my eyes closed, trying to shut out the world. Marie waited impatiently, wanting to know the worst and having it over with, or be able to fix it.

"Robin." Damn. My ears were still working.

"Look at me Robin. Open your eyes," M. Bordeau said gently.

Reluctantly, I opened my eyes and looked at him in fear. "Robin, there has been a terrible accident at the school." He said this very quietly and gently.

Oh, no, please no, I prayed. I started to cry. Just when I thought I couldn't take anymore, I got more.

"Please don't tell me. Please, I'll do anything not to know," I pleaded. I was shaking all over and sobbing. Marie tried to put her arm around me, and I pushed her away. "I don't deserve this! I didn't do anything that would make me deserve more pain." I was angry and tired. Why didn't the world find someone else to pick on?

Jack Bordeau came off his chair and shook me. "Listen to me, Robin! You have to be strong one more time. I didn't wish this on you, and I would do anything not to be the one to tell you, but there is a situation. Go wash your face and blow your nose. Mary, make some coffee and bring out the bottle of brandy. Put some in a cup with coffee for me and Robin, and we will brace ourselves."

I went to the bathroom and did as I was told, trying to prolong the trip back to the kitchen. Eventually, I returned. The coffee tasted strange with brandy in it, and I didn't like it much, but it did seem to warm me inside. I thought that it might immediately render me comatose and let me avoid life for a while. Unfortunately, there wasn't enough brandy in the coffee to do more than warm my throat.

When he thought I was calm enough to hear the news, M. Bordeau took a deep breath and said, "That was the school. They tried to call your mother, but I guess she was out. Your brother Peter was found early this morning in the shower. He had a cord around his neck, and he was hanging from the shower head." He said this all in a rush, not wanting to prolong the pain. He stopped speaking and moved his chair close to mine. He put his arm around my shoulder.

I was numb. I didn't hurt. I didn't feel anything. I wasn't angry. I was dead inside. "I guess they have been trying to call here all morning, but no one answered. You must have been very sound asleep." M. Bordeau continued talking, but I didn't hear him. I just stared unseeingly at nothing.

"Jack, he's in shock," said Marie.

A glass was pressed against my lips, and the fumes from straight brandy assailed my nostrils, making them smart. My cheek stung as M. Bordeau slapped it. I focused long enough to see him standing over me. I could smell burnt eggs. I felt myself being lifted and carried to my room. I fell into a dreamless sleep and woke up the next morning to Marie hovering over me.

"Oh, good, you are awake," she said with a sigh of relief.

I didn't think that it was so good. I wanted to go back to unconsciousness. I started to rock myself, hoping for sleep to return. Instead, I became more awake. There was no escape.

"Some men from the school will be bringing your brother Paul here. They should be here soon. Jack is outside in the barn feeding the chickens," Marie said nervously.

Paul! I hadn't even thought about him. Oh my god! What must he be going through? I nodded dumbly at Marie and tried to summon up the strength to get out of bed. I had been in the same clothes forever, it seemed. I felt dirty and wanted a bath.

Marie must have read my mind. "You are pretty high smelling, Robin. Why don't I draw you a bath, and you have a good long soak. Your other jeans are clean and dry. There is a fresh shirt and sweater in the drawer along with clean socks and underwear."

She left the room and let me stagger out of bed. I sat on the edge of the bed, feeling a little dizzy and weak. Marie came back with a towel and said, "Take those clothes off and wrap this around you. Everything, including your bedding, is going in the washing machine."

I obediently did as I was told and soaked in the tub until the water had turned cold. I ran some more hot water and began to wash. My mouth tasted awful, and my hair was glued to my head. I slid down in the water, submerging my head, and then surfaced to wash my hair. I felt a little better as I brushed my teeth. When I went back through the kitchen on the way to my pantry room, I heard M. Bordeau walking around on the veranda. Shortly after, I heard tires on the gravel in the drive, and moments later, M. Bordeau was speaking to someone.

I was in the kitchen on a chair, not knowing what I should be doing or where I should be. Paul came in, followed by Brother Gordon and Uncle Alvin. Paul's face was grim, his jaw was clenched, and his body tense. He seemed to be flexing every muscle in his body and ready to fight.

I stayed in my seat, waiting to be told what to do. I felt no friendliness toward the school director, and my feelings toward Uncle Alvin were confused. Until I left the school, he had been my friend, solace, and salvation; when I returned the other day, he treated me like an exile.

My anger over Peter had not surfaced yet. M. Bordeau, however, was not even trying to be civil. He was purple with rage and pulled Paul over beside me on the other side of the room.

"Robin, I am sure that you and Paul will want to talk. Why don't you go into the front room while I have a word with these gentlemen?"

He turned to Marie and asked, "Can you take Nikki somewhere?"

Marie lifted Nikki out of his chair and said, "Come on, honey, I think it's time we sorted out your toy chest."

Paul and I went into the front room and sat down, not knowing what to say to each other. I wasn't ready for information about Peter.

In the kitchen, we could hear M. Bordeau's raised voice. "What kind of place are you running over there? Are you not supposed to be nurturing these boys? How can a mere child hang himself?" With each word, his voice became a decibel louder.

Brother Gordon's voice was just a mumble.

"Don't think that I am going to let you sweep this thing under the rug. If the boy was withdrawn, why was he not being watched—counseled?"

"There are two hundred boys at the school." The director's voice had become an audible whine. "We can't watch all of them all the time. Sometimes, quiet depression goes unnoticed."

From my position in the front room, Brother Gordon had taken on a different character. He no longer seemed the formidable force that ran the school, but a sniveling weakling.

"Then you should not be in charge of them if you are unable to run the place as it was meant to be run. Supposedly wiser men than I decided that these boys, and all the others in your school, would be better served and have a better chance at life for being there. In the past, the boys you have sent to me have sometimes intimated that there was an element of cruelty at the school, but I always passed that off as their interpretation of discipline. This week, I have heard stories that can only have me believe that you are running a place that is no better than a Nazi prisoner of war camp! My god! What kind of church have I believed in all these years? What kind of sadistic and satanic place is that school?" His voiced cracked, and his faith crumbled.

Uncle Alvin's voice came through the door, but I couldn't make out the words.

"I will make sure that these boys get home. Then I will blow you and your school to kingdom come!" M. Bordeau was screaming now. "Now get the hell out of my house!"

Shortly after, the back door slammed, and I heard the engine of the car start, and the wheels crunch the gravel in the laneway. I stood at the window and watched as it drove down the road. M. Bordeau stood at the side of the lane and watched after it, not moving. Marie came through the front room with Nikki in her arms and went into the kitchen. I looked at Paul and jerked my head in the direction of the kitchen.

When the four of us were in the kitchen, the back door opened, and a very troubled M. Bordeau came in. Marie went to him and put her arms around him.

"Maybe we should have a nice cup of cocoa," she said.

CPSIA information can be obtained at www.ICGtesting.com
Printed in the USA
LVOW130011221212
312821LV00001B/4/P